The Lady's Masked Mistake

Laura Osborne

DEDICATION

For Mae,

May we never stop finding ways to laugh at each other

Prologue

The Joys of Gossip

There are many facts known to the "good" people of the ton that the commonfolk would find no use for. For instance, if an unwed woman (especially one in possession of her maidenhead) were to find herself alone in a room with a man of no relation to her, she would be thoroughly compromised. And although the risk of this happening to the maidens of a good family is feared, it will not stop said family from hosting a lavish masquerade ball in the hopes that an unrelated maiden should be ruined.

For when it comes to those "good" gentlefolk of the ton, nothing is more wonderful to the ears than a scandal or a rumour. But even more delicious for these salacious folks, is the pleasure of being a witness to a scene and therefore being able to spread the word to others under the pretence of shock and disgust.

The best entertainment, of course, can be attributed to the noble families of Ainsworth and Wexford. Indeed, gossip surrounding these two families spreads like wildfire. Most notably over the course of the past few years. However, before

I begin to regale you with the sensations of the two houses, I must thoroughly introduce you to them.

We shall first examine the similarities between the families; The Ainsworth's hold the Dukedom of Bristol, whilst the neighbouring Duchy of Gloucester is held by Wexford's. His Lordship Geoffrey Ainsworth, Duke of Bristol married Lady Verity Fredericks at the dawn of the 1785 season and at the end of the season, James Wexford, Duke of Gloucester married Miss Cora Fraser. Much to the chagrin of Lord Bristol, he and his wife took longer to conceive than the Gloucester's. Both couples welcomed their eldest son's on the 23rd of April 1786. To the satisfaction of Lord Bristol, the young Lord William Ainsworth was born at seven o'clock in the morning, preceding Lord Matthew Wexford by twelve hours, thirty-seven minutes, and fifteen seconds, to be exact as Lord Bristol must be in a matter such as this.

Both families stopped growing in the year 1792, first with the birth of Lady Constance Wexford and last with the arrival of Lord Frederick Ainsworth. Both families produced four children each who were deeply bonded. And this is where the commonalities end.

The Ainsworth's were an ancient noble line, dating back to the Norman invasion, fuelling the pride of their ancestry. The more vulgar observers would often say that their golden hair was only outshined by goldenness emerging from their derrieres. Their fair complexion indeed would often stress the Duchess to no ends trying to keep the girls out of the sun lest they burn.

Although the marriage of the Duke of Duchess produced four children, most onlookers would be forgiven for assuming that they had five. For from the tender age of five years, Miss Marie Ainsworth, the orphaned niece of the Duke, joined her cousins in Ainsley Manor, planting herself firmly in the middle of the "big pair" of Liam and Colette and the "little pair" of Eliza and Freddie.

The Wexford's were of much newer stock, having gained their title just one hundred years prior thanks to a childhood friendship between the first Duke of Gloucester and the new king William III. Considered more practical and possessed of less snobbery than their ancient counterparts, the current generation of Wexford's are the first of their line to be considered true members of the ton.

The arrivals of the four Wexford children have often been remarked by members of the ton as fully reflecting of their family's practicality. Duncan followed Matt's birth two years later, two years after Duncan came Harry, who was in the same amount of time followed by Connie. Each child possessed the dark colouring of their parents and would often find some way of hinting their Scottish ancestry on their person.

The families would often come across each other when out in society and maintained an aura of polished politeness when in conversation with one another. But altogether the two families ensured they kept their distance from one another lest they give the ton reasons to set their tongues wagging. Eyes of the ton would always be on the two families, itching for any sort of scandal or dispute between the two.

For this was another fact of the ton that few outside of the society cared for. The Ainsworth's of Bristol and the Wexford's of Gloucester completely and utterly detested one another. Without a doubt it is a good thing the two families resolved to stay away from one another. Of course, with two families with beautiful and eligible lords and ladies in society at the same time what could possibly happen?

Chapter One

April 18th, 1809

"I'm telling you Fawcett; you are getting yourself an angel."
Duncan Wexford sent his sister, Connie, the cheekiest wink to
accompany his teasing.

The pair were sat in the sitting room of their
Kensington home where they, along with their mother and
eldest brother, were entertaining Connie's fiancé, Sir Ernest
Fawcett.

Connie struggled to prevent herself rolling her blue
eyes at her brother's comment. Instead, she maintained her
composure and flashed her eyes towards her fiancé.

"Please, Ernest, do not listen to my silly older brother.
I am far from the angel he's suggesting."

"Oh please," chimed in Matt, their eldest brother, "I
don't think I've ever seen or heard of you misbehaving in the
seventeen years I have been forced to endure your company."

Ernest, to his credit Connie noted, humoured her brothers. Chuckling as he sent her a dazzling look.

"Why else should you suppose I asked your delightful sister to be my wife. I shall never have to worry about having to get her out of any trouble and she truly shall be the perfect hostess in society."

"Exactly as her father and I raised her," Cora, Duchess of Gloucester contributed to the conversation, "how we achieved this I do not know. With three older brothers and her closest female relatives' miles away, it is a miracle our lovely Connie never tried to follow the boys on their rough activities."

A miracle indeed, thought Connie, when one considers it almost did not turn out that way! She could still remember visiting her uncle William when she was six years old. Her cousins, Anne and Victoria, could barely hold back their shock at how quickly she could climb a tree and how eager she was to go on jaunts in the muddiest patches of their gardens.

Seeing the prim and proper way her cousins had silently voiced their disapproval compelled Connie to request as much education in becoming a true society lady as possible upon her return home. She recalled the disappointment in Harry's expression when she began refusing to join the boys on their excursions.

The lessons had served her well though. After a whirlwind courtship in her very first season, Connie had become the first debutante to be engaged, much to the envy of her fellow debs. She felt great relief that she would not have to refuse any offers of marriage. Ernest had been the ideal match she had aimed for prior to her debut: The tall, dark-haired, blue-eyed war hero was as handsome as he was rich, and Connie knew she would always be well cared for.

"My darling," her fiancé interrupted her musings, "pay no heed to your brothers. I would much rather have a well-behaved wife than the naughty minx of a sister your brothers wish you were." The palm of Connie's hand tingled at the soft stroke of his fingers as he sought to reassure her.

"Well, I'm sure you'll bring out a naughty side of her if you're any good a husband."

"Duncan, your jests go too far," chided Cora, "I am afraid Constance and I must leave to prepare for our visit to the dressmakers Sir Ernest. We will see you at the Coleman ball tonight though of course."

Before Ernest could respond, a loud groan came from the chaise. Four heads turned to observe Matt's hitting the back of the furniture with a thud.

"I say old chap, I thought you were the party animal of the Wexford clan." Ernest could not wipe the incredulous look off his face. Matt's only response was to close his eyes and groan even further.

"It's not so much fun when your invitation is accompanied by the threat of castration." Chuckled Duncan.

"I cannot think of worse torture than having to attend a masquerade ball hosted by Viscountess Coleman where I shall have to coo and pretend to be blissfully in love with a total stranger."

"That stranger happens to be your wife Matthew," Cora once again being forced to chastise one of her sons, "and let us not forget that the only reason why you do not have any familiarity with her is entirely of your own doing."

Connie felt the familiar pain of sympathy for dear Jane. The beauty was four years her senior and for the past two years since her wedding she had had to suffer the mocking eyes of the entire ton, no doubt fully aware of the couple's estrangement since practically the wedding itself.

"Well do not doubt Connie darling, I shall never complain at the prospect of spending any time with you. In fact, I plan to scarcely leave your side after our vows."

Connie felt butterflies in her stomach at Ernest's declaration. The look of Duncan's face suggested he also had a feeling in his but a remarkably less pleasant one.

Rather than face any further mocking from her brothers, the ladies took their leave to their rooms to prepare for their trip to the dressmakers.

Later in the evening, Connie sat at her dressing table smiling to herself as Letitia went about preparing her hair for the ball. She had planned the evening meticulously since her mother had come to her the day after the engagement to prepare her for what to expect upon her marriage.

As her raven curls were pinned into a twist, Connie observed her reflection. She had often bemoaned not inheriting the stark green eyes of her mother but given the right styles, her dark blue eyes could be quite striking. It was for this reason that she had chosen to wear a soft yellow dress and matching mask to the ball. She had often been complimented on the colour and was often compared to a Spanish lady rather than Scottish like her mother.

A slight tinge of rouge was added to her plump lips. It took much convincing to get Letitia to agree but it was simply necessary for her plan to work tonight.

Thinking back to the conversation in the sitting room today widened Connie's smile even further. Her brothers had no idea the plan she had put in motion: Ernest had told her that he would be wearing a blue flower in his lapel tonight (to match her eyes). She planned to somehow thrust a note into his hand containing directions to a small portrait room in the Coleman house.

The one regret Connie had about her first season being such an immediate success was that she was unable to steal secret kisses or clandestine meetings before her engagement and, as luck would have it, she managed to find herself engaged to perhaps the most noble man in the ton. A man who would not have dreamed of suggesting anything scandalous. So, it was down to her to arrange for them to have a little excitement before the wedding.

She could not keep the butterflies in the pit of her stomach at bay as Connie thought of the two achievements tonight would bring: Her first kiss and Ernest would have the pleasure of seeing what a minx he would have in his bed once they had married!

Chapter Two

The atmosphere at Coleman House was the most intense it had been all season. It appeared to Connie as she walked into the ballroom on the arm of her youngest brother, Harry, that every single person was glimpsing around trying to ascertain who was behind each mask and who they would be having a secret rendezvous with later. The latter thought caused her smile to tilt upwards as she searched the room for her blue flower.

"You are up to something sister!" Connie turned to see the impishness in Harry's emerald eyes as he looked down at her, smirking. "And if you ask me, I'd say it's going to be rather enjoyable."

Connie could not help but laugh at her brother's cheekiness "If I'm up to something then you are up to *everything* and I cannot wait to find out what it is."

"I shouldn't hope to guess what you are referring to. I am a perfect gentleman and have no desire to cause any mischief."

"Oh please, I don't recall a single event I have attended all season where you have been present and not done something to disturb the peace for your own amusement."

With his hand clasped to his chest in faux shock Harry elected to sound as if he would burst into tears at any moment "You wound me my dearest sister," "Only sister" "shh I am trying to play the innocent for once in my life."

Upon seeing the ridiculing expression on Connie's face, Harry gave up his pretence and laughed. "Oh fine, you'll find out soon enough. In fact, the sooner I turn you over to my actual dearest sister I can enact my wicked schemes."

"Don't mock Jane like that" Connie could not help but admonish her brother "she has enough to deal with the humiliation of Matt's rejection without your teasing to add to it!" At that they were suddenly brought to a halt as Harry turned to her, suddenly serious.

"Do you honestly think she prefers your obvious pity? Jane does very well without Matt's attentions on her. Once you have been in society as long as I have, you will begin to notice that men fall over each other in the hopes of getting her attention. Just because our eldest brother is the biggest fool in all of the Ton does not mean that everyone else is and Janey knows that to embrace that is the best revenge she can......are you even listening to me?"

No, she was not. In fact, very shortly into her brother's pseudo-lecture, Connie had glimpsed the very thing she was looking for: A blue flower on a gentleman's lapel. Ernest had since turned his back, evidently not spying his betrothed standing nearby, but even so she could feel the intense heat of his person.

Upon seeing the curious look Harry was giving her Connie frantically glanced around for a distraction. "Oh look, there's Jane over there and Matt is with her too. We must go to them now. You would never forgive yourself for neglecting to tease them!"

Somehow managing to gracefully push Harry over to their relations, Connie took the note she had hidden and gently pressed it into the palm of her betrothed as they strolled past him. Feeling relief at the brief touch of his fingers pressing to the note, she turned to Harry, "Well are you going to tell me your plan for tonight or….?"

Her escort couldn't help but smirk "You'll see soon enough, in fact, Matt being here makes in even more perfect. Tonight, shall be my greatest triumph."

"I don't want to know do I?" Connie heard Jane utter, having not realised that they had reached their destination.

"I certainly don't know what you're talking about." Harry gently took his sister's hand and passed it into the crook of Matt's arm. "Well, I've done my bit and now must deposit it into your care as I have urgent business to attend to."

"IT?"

"Henry James Wexford what are you about to do?" Matt's questioning became more frantic as Harry grinned, bowed, and turned. "Harry the last time you tried something the Prince of Wales was almost doused in syrup......Harry......Harry......That boy is going to be the death of me!"

Barely able to conceal her grin, Jane turned to her husband, "Do not worry my darling husband, I'm sure your brother will not be committing treason tonight. He wouldn't dare at my mother's ball; he likes me far too much."

Upon seeing the venom in the pair's eyes as they looked at each other, Connie hastened to change the topic of conversation. "You look utterly beautiful tonight Jane; the colour suits you so."

Connie could safely admit to herself that she was not lying. Although her delicate features were hidden behind her mask, Jane could never be missed by her flame-red hair and the pairing of the deep green silk truly made her a vision to behold. If only her husband could see it.

"I should say the same to you too Constance, I am so glad you took my advice and picked the yellow gown. Indeed, the contrast of your mask truly brings out how vivi...."

The pause in Jane's words caused both the eldest and youngest Wexford siblings to follow her gaze and shortly afterwards all three had dropped their jaws in surprise at what they saw.

"Oh, please say he isn't!"

"He's going to get himself killed!"

"Everyone is going to be talking about this!"

Indeed, they would, for every person in the ballroom had turned their heads towards Lord Henry Wexford as he approached a golden-haired beauty in soft pink and held out his hand in request of a dance.

The silence in the room was so great that all that could be heard was the light pattering of rain on the windows. No one could take their eyes off the couple. Slowly, the lady placed her hand within his and allowed Harry to lead her to the dance floor.

All at once animated chatter consumed the ballroom as everyone turned to one another to discuss this new development. Everyone, that is, except for Connie, Matt, and Jane, who all looked as if they had the wind thoroughly knocked out of them.

The first to break out of their stupor was Jane, who turned to her husband and in hushed but panicked tones pleaded with him "Please, Matthew. Whatever you do, do not do it here and now. Wait until the ball is over and then speak with him."

Matt closed his eyes as he brought his fingers to the bridge of his nose. "He has gone too far this time Jane. If I don't tell him papa certainly will." Throwing his hands in the air, Matt could not stop himself from exclaiming "Of all the idiotic, selfish, hair-brained ideas that boy has ever had, why in god's name would he go and dance with Elizabeth Ainsworth?"

Ten minutes earlier

Alexander Chalmers, Earl of Sutton had been at the Coleman ball for only six minutes, and he had already decided it would be a complete an utter bore. Stood with his oldest friend, Robert Calvert, he could not help bemoaning how obvious the young, unmarried ladies of the ton were being.

With an exasperated look, he turned to Calvert, "Do you think they practiced these 'alluring' looks in the mirror before tonight?" Calvert could not help but chuckle as he responded "I think they're under the impression that wearing a mask suddenly makes them a temptress and do not realise that us older, experienced men can see through their little act."

Of course, that was it, Xander realised, the few times he has attended masquerade balls the atmosphere was always filled with a sense of apprehension at what mischief people could get up to. It was why he tried his best to avoid them, a sudden engagement almost always appeared the following morning and the groom-to-be never looked too excited at the prospect of marriage.

"The day I fall for one of these foolish schemes of faux-coquettes you have permission to remove me from this earth."

"And that shall truly be the day you make my dreams come true Sutton." Calvert's gaze suddenly became fixed upon the entrance of the ballroom, "At last the entertainment has arrived."

Following Calvert's gaze, Xander saw the Ainsworth's had just arrived and were making their way over to them. Liam Ainsworth, the future Duke of Bristol, had attended university with Xander and Calvert and the three of them had practically become brothers, despite their different upbringings.

One the outset, Robert Calvert was the most different of the three men. A businessman who, like his father before him, somehow knew where the money was before anyone else did, no matter the venture. This meant the ton could not ignore him, despite his lack of aristocratic upbringing, but they ensured he knew their true opinion of him through their not-so-subtle barbs. Xander and Liam embracing him as one of their own, on the other hand, meant that they were the only one's Calvert was willing to share his financial knowledge with, making them two of the richest members of the ton.

Although Xander and Liam were two born and bred members of the ton, they could not have experienced more different upbringings. Although Liam's father, the Duke of Bristol, had a reputation of coldness to all, his own family would have a different story to tell. They grew up in a loving household and never felt uncomfortable in their own skin.

Xander had always felt that he never belonged in his family. His father, the late Earl of Sutton, was cold and distant and his mother, whom he begrudgingly supported in her extravagant lifestyle, was even more absent a parent, if that were possible. Xander hated his own reflection as a result, seeing his mother's dark blue eyes and raven black hair combined with the strong jaw and sharp cheekbones of his father reminded him of everything he hated in his life.

Much to his joy, Xander found himself embraced by the Ainsworths as if he were one of their own and for the first time in his life, Xander had begun to find himself at peace with himself. Of course, he still had a deep mistrust of other members of the ton. But he had the comfort of knowing he had his own safe space and, although he never voiced it, Xander had the distinct feeling that Calvert felt the same.

Grinning to himself, Xander knew Calvert had another reason why he should be so fond of the Ainsworth family and he was about to use it, much to his friend's chagrin.

Liam approached with two beauties on his arm, his sister, Eliza, and his cousin, Marie. The three of them together dazzling with their golden countenances. Eliza, as usual, looked ravishing in a soft pink but it was Marie who Xander directed his attentions to.

"Miss Ainsworth, I must say that blue looks particularly fetching on you, so fetching in fact that I am afraid I must do this......" Xander promptly leaned over and plucked a flower from her hair. As he took to the task of attaching it to his suit jacket, he could see from the corner of his eye the hard stare Calvert was giving him.

Turning his attentions back to Marie, Xander could not help but notice she did not seem pleased to have received such intimate attention and felt a pang of guilt at using her to rile his friend up.

"You should feel so lucky darling cousin," everyone's attentions turned to Eliza, "I have tried so hard to get His Lordship to marry me and officially become one of the family, but he won't even give me a compliment on my dress."

Clasping his hands behind him and laughing, Xander did not need to respond as Liam decided to take his sister to task. "Perhaps Sutton had noticed, like the rest of us already have, that you are by far the vainest member of the family and need to be given a lesson in humility." Upon seeing his sister's scowl, he added, "Not to mention, Marie does look beautiful, and she just needs people to tell her more, so she believes it herself." He finished by directing a wink to his cousin.

"Marie always looks beautiful," Eliza countered, always having to have the last word, "and unlike the three of you I make sure I always tell her that." It did not escape Xander's notice that she gave Calvert a pointed look as she spoke. *Of course, she would have worked it out too.*

"Do I get a say in all of this or shall I just let you all discuss me as though I were not here?" Marie contributed to the conversation with an uncharacteristically harsh tone.

Xander frowned, realising that they had all probably made the naturally shy Marie even more self-conscious than she usually was at events like this. However, his thoughts and attentions were suddenly interrupted by the feel of a slip of paper being gently pressed against his hand.

Instinctively, he grasped the note but when he turned around, he could not see anyone that he knew (not that you could tell with the masks everyone was wearing). Additionally, there did not appear to be anyone looking at him or seeming as if they had reached out.

Feeling more curious by the second, Xander opened the note and read:

My Darling,

I cannot wait to be alone with you.

Go down the hall from the ladies dressing room, turn left and take the third door on the right.

I will be waiting for you. Please do not disappoint me!

Always yours,

C

Furrowing his brows, Xander could not decide if he was more irritated at the prospect of being lured into some marriage trap or at the thought of a lover of his deciding to play a game of cat and mouse.

Tucking the note in his pocket, Xander tried to work out who the mysterious C could be. It was a popular letter to begin a woman's name at the current time. God knows how many Charlottes or Caroline's were running about. It could also be her surname; they were after all at the Coleman ball.

Alternatively, C could be related to a title. Xander mentally listed some of them off: Chester......Cumberland......Cambridge. But of all these options, who could it be to want to invite him to a private liaison. Unless......

There was one lady, an actress, to whom Xander was acquainted very well. Under normal circumstances, she would never be able to attend any event held by the Ton but a masquerade ball, where no one would know the difference.

Xander grinned to himself. Miss Antonia Maltby, more commonly known to those intimately close to her as Coco. They had enjoyed an affair on and off throughout the years and she truly was a delectable lover. This godforsaken party may be enjoyable after all.

Xander was brought out of his musings by a sudden hissing noise made next to him. Turning to his friend, he noted with surprise that he had never seen such an angry look in his eyes before. Drawing his gaze upon the rest of his companions, he knew something was wrong. The rosy cheeks that Marie usually sported had gone a ghostly white and Calvert's jaw was uncommonly ajar. And Eliza was..........

Where the devil has Eliza gone?

Searching the ballroom, he quickly spotted her enjoying a waltz. Rather thoroughly enjoying a waltz if you asked his opinion. Her dancing partner was tall and had chestnut locks. But this, Xander considered, was no indication of who he might be. Indeed, a good portion of his face was covered in a mask. Not one too different to his own.

"Who is that chap dancing with Eliza?" Xander regretted asking the question as soon as he heard the name come out of Liam's mouth.

"Harry Wexford."

Oh god!

Chapter Three

Harry's little mischief making plot surprisingly worked out to Connie's advantage. Immediately after the waltz had finished, Matt had ushered him into the library with Jane following behind to try and calm the situation. Connie quickly saw her chance to sneak out of the ballroom to the portrait gallery.

The room was smaller than most galleries, during the summer it was used by the Colemans for painting as the windows overlooked the gardens. Stepping in front of one of the windows, Connie basked in the moonlight. It was the only source of light in the room, making it far more romantic for its purpose tonight.

Connie could feel his presence rather than see or hear him. Still facing the window, Connie shut her eyes as she spoke. "I know it isn't proper to be here alone. But I needed to be with you…...to feel you…....just one time…...before it is too late."

He did not speak. Normally, she would not be able to bear the silence of the room but on this occasion, it was thrilling. The heat and anticipation seemed to consume everything around her.

Connie felt his hands suddenly appear on her waist, jolting her senses. She had not heard his approach. His thumbs made gentle circles that scorched her through her dress. Slowly, one of his hands lifted to stroke a finger down the side of her neck. Slowly, torturously drifting down until it met the top of her dress.

She leant back against his hard chest as she gave in to his movements. The magnetism of his body consumed her. In the haze of her mind, she realised that she would give him anything and everything he wanted there and then. Her intention for tonight was only for a kiss but with barely a touch he dominated her very being and she needed more.

When his lips made contact with her shoulder Connie could not help but gasp, she hadn't realised that he had undone the buttons of her dress. As his lips drifted up her neck in the softest of kisses, he lowered her dress until her chest was bared, hardening her nipples in the cool air.

Raising his hand once again, he held her chin and turned her head to the side, finally taking her mouth with his.

He started off with slow, gentle pecks which gradually sped up as the passion between them began to erupt. He licked and nibbled her lips. Sensing what he wanted, Connie opened her mouth to him, tentatively meeting his tongue with hers as it entered and explored her mouth.

She could not stop herself moaning into his mouth as his hands came up to cup her breasts. They teased her.

Stroking the sides of her breasts and lifting his fingers so that her nipples passed through them.

The second he began to stroke her nipples she felt her womanhood stir in desperate need. Their kiss grew frantic and the desperate need to consume one another took over. He turned her to face him, tearing his lips from hers. Before she could protest the loss, Connie gasped as he took one of her nipples into his mouth, flicking the bud it found there.

She could not help the whimpers that escaped her lips as he alternated between her breasts. The feel of his mouth sucking, nibbling, and tasting drained her of all coherent thoughts. She ran her hands through his hair while his clasped her buttocks through her dress. It was then that she felt the hardness of him, she could not stop her hips from thrusting against his in desperate need of relief as her arousal grew.

"Take me!" She moaned under hooded eyelashes. He released her nipple and lifted his head to meet her gaze. The desire she saw in his eyes was so deep that Connie thought it turned the blue of his eyes so dark they were almost black.

Taking her mouth in another scorching kiss, he clenched his hands around her buttocks, lifting her to push her against the nearest wall.

The need between the two of them became frantic. As their tongues clashed in a desperate hunger for one another, Connie felt her skirts being lifted and the front slit of her drawers being torn larger.

The second she felt his finger brush against her folds she tore her mouth from his to moan. His finger stroked her until the slickness coming from her quim was coating him. His thumbs had begun making circles around her bud, sending shockwaves of pleasure through her entire body.

His mouth found a spot on her neck which only increased the pleasure, distracted her from the strange sensation that came as his fingers entered and stretched her. All coherent thoughts had been stripped from mind other than one word, that she could not help but moan at him.

"More..........more..........oh god please, I need more."

His head lifted, his intense gaze meeting hers. Just underneath the black mask he had donned she could see the smirk on his lips. Suddenly, he grasped her thighs, lifting her as he thrust into her heat.

Gasping at the sudden pain, Connie's muscles clenched around him. The pain began to ebb away as the pleasure of this deep thrusts took over and, once again, Connie could not help but moan at the power he unleashed.

Her tightness was excruciatingly blissful.

The confusion Xander had felt when he first saw the unexpected woman in the moonlight had quickly vanished as he had drawn his eyes over her form.

Raven black hair and the most delectable curves enraptured him and the invitations she kept making towards him had only spurred him on even more. At each moment of discovery of each part of her body he felt his cock grow harder and harder and he felt he would burst the moment his fingers made contact with her heat and he felt how wet she was.

She was dripping for him.

He had intended on going slow but the second he entered her, he became overtaken with a lust even more maddening than before.

Burying his head in his lover's neck, Xander thrust as deep and hard as he could. Sensing he was going to come quickly, he needed to bring her to the brink of desire with him.

Letting go of one of her legs, he brought his hand to her clit, stroking her in time with his thrusts. Sensing she was about to peak, he leant his forehead against hers, staring into her eyes and embracing the intensity he felt reflecting back at his.

Muffling her scream with his mouth when she tipped over the edge, Xander felt her walls clench around him, bringing him to his release. All the while his mind was encapsulated with one thing: *Mine*

Xander did not know who this mysterious woman was or why she wanted him here tonight, but he did not care. He was going to make sure she remained his. God, he needed her sprawled naked in his bed as he pleasured her until all she knew that she belonged to him and him alone.

Letting her go, Xander leaned his head against the wall next to hers desperately trying to get his breath under control. Before he could stop her, she slid out from underneath him and ran from the room.

Readjusting his clothing, Xander hastened to follow her but as he left the gallery and looked down the hall, he could not see her anywhere. Somehow, he maintained a calm demeanour as he walked back to the ballroom, his eyes searching the room for his mysterious woman.

Not finding her anywhere, Xander made his way back towards his companions, barely taking in the obvious tenseness of the group owing to Eliza's impromptu dance with the Wexford boy. Calvert spotted him first.

"I say, where did you get to Sutton?" Then, taking in his friend's demeanour, "well at least one of us enjoyed themselves." He chortled.

Three pairs of eyes rapidly turned to him. Realising there was no use feigning ignorance amongst this group, Xander instead chose to take advantage of them all.

"Is there any chance any of you have seen a dark-haired lady in a dress of…..." *Oh god,* he hadn't even been able to properly see what colour she wore in the dark of the room, "some sort of…uh…. I think it was orange."

"Orange?" Eliza scoffed "If I had seen a woman wearing orange I would have noticed!"

Marie tried to help the situation "Maybe it was a related colour? A red or yellow perhaps?" Xander could not believe his bad luck, pinching the bridge of his nose trying to bring his thoughts in order, a sudden silence took over the group and he thought he heard one of the women gasp.

Looking at his friends faces, for the second time that night he realised something major had happened. Liam was the one to give voice to what they were all thinking.

"Please tell me you cut your finger." The blood drained from Xander's face.

Slowly turning his gaze downward, Xander looked in horror at his fingers. There was the unmistakeable sight of blood and he was sure that when he undressed for bed that night he would be greeted by a familiar sight on his cock.

"Oh god. What have I done?"

Chapter Four

Xander woke up the following morning with a headache and an acute sense of dread. The former he could attribute to the entire bottle of whiskey he and Calvert had shared to commiserate his situation whilst the latter was directed towards the brunch invitation he had previously accepted from Verity Ainsworth, Duchess of Bristol and more of a mother to him than his own mother.

Owing to this relationship, he would not be able to escape the event. As his valet attempted to make him presentable for the day, the hangover he was sporting was causing him to make uncomfortable groaning noises whenever he would move. This was not an optimistic start to the day.

Making his way down the stairs of his Mayfair townhouse, Xander heard the distinct sound of female chatter and grimaced, remembering that his mother and her catty group of society witches were in the drawing room engaging in their favourite sport of gossiping about the events of the previous night.

Slowing down his pace, Xander tiptoed towards the front door hoping to escape by unseen. Unfortunately, he appeared to be going through an unlucky streak as four steps away from the door he heard the ear-splitting shriek:

"SUTTTTTOOOOOOONNNNNNN!!!"

Wincing at his misfortune, he turned and made his way towards the coven already preparing his escape plan.

"Good Morning Mother" then turning to the rest of them with a bow "Ladies. I am afraid I cannot linger as I have an appointment that I cannot be late for."

"I should think your poor, lonely mother would take precedence over the Ainsworth clan." Helena Chalmers, the Dowager Countess of Sutton venomously stated, her eyes narrowing towards her eldest son. "After all, I was the one who birthed you. Surely that awards some form of companionship for me."

Eyeing the other ladies in the room it took all his willpower not to roll his eyes at her, "My apologies Mother, I did not think you would need my company when you have all your *lovely* lady friends here with you." And if he remained, he was sure they would try to accost him into their beds when her back was turned as they usually attempted.

The slim chance any of them had was gone in any case. Or at least would be once he found his mystery lover.

With the sickliest of grins plastered across her face, the Dowager Countess held her hand out for her son to kiss. "I suppose I should forgive you in this instance. Do give my fondest wishes to the family, especially young Eliza. Such a beauty. I'm sure she would be a lovely addition to the household......If you understand my meaning."

Eyebrows raised in amusement as his mother's obviousness, Xander released her hand. "Alas, I may just disappoint you in that wish Mother dear. Good day ladies."

With that final statement, Xander promptly turned and left the room, now more irritated than he had been when he awoke an hour earlier. He almost paused as he prepared to walk out the door when he heard one of the witches loudly declare her opinion of the matter.

"Well, I suppose no one will want her now. The way Harry Wexford was looking at her gave me the distinct impression that the girl follows through on her flirtations."

Anger surging through him at the crass manner at which they were gossiping over Eliza, Xander resisted the urge to stride back in the room and pummel the woman. Instead, he walked into the fresh air, promptly forgetting his anger as the sudden movement caused a bout a nausea and he proceeded to vomit all over his mother's prized hydrangeas.

At approximately the same time the Earl of Sutton was publicly emptying the contents of his stomach, Connie and her maid were making their way to Hyde Park where she had arranged to meet with Sir Ernest for a morning stroll.

She had awoken that morning feeling blissfully confident that her impending marriage would be much more enjoyable than she had originally anticipated. As her maid helped her into a blue day dress, Connie could not keep the smile of her face and had to play coy at the breakfast table with her family. Most of them seemed to be too enraptured in their own discussions to notice, especially when the topic of Harry's dance the night before came up. However, Connie perceived Duncan directing suspicious looks her way. After all, she considered, if any of her brothers were to notice anything, it would be him.

As they waited to meet Ernest, she replayed the events of the previous night in her head. The passion shared between the two was unlike any she had ever expected. Indeed, she had found Ernest pleasing to look at from the off, but this just amazed her.

"My darling, I do hope you haven't been waiting here long." Connie was brought out of her daydream by the object of her thoughts. She was suddenly overcome with shyness and warmth began to spread in her cheeks.

Chuckling, Ernest took her hand, placed it in the crook of his elbow and lead her along the riverside. Connie debated internally as to how to lead the conversation into their activities the previous night.

"I must utter my apologies for last night," Ernest took the step for her, "I do hope you will not think too low of me." Noticing the pleading look in his eyes, Connie was taken by surprise. Why should he be so repentant over their liaison? She was to be his wife and seemed very much to enjoy himself.

Of course, she realised, other than last night Ernest had always endeavoured to remain a true gentleman. He would naturally be horrified at how carried away they had become. Connie placed her free hand upon his arm to reassure him.

"Do not fret, my love. I am the one to blame after all."

"Why should you be blamed at all? It's not your fault my foolish sister decided to have her child earlier than expected!"

Confusion spread over both their features.

"What do you mean?" Connie implored.

"She had a rather troubled labour, but she and her new son have come through it rather well."

"I am glad to hear it but what does that have to do with last night?" A sense of dread began to take root in the pit of her stomach.

Ernest furrowed his brows in confusion, "Well, it's why I was not able to attend the ball last night. Naturally, I would have been by your side if it had not been for Bess."

Oh god.

Connie's mind began to spin as it processed what he was saying. Denial began to overtake her. Perhaps he was jesting. After all, Connie had clearly misbehaved by giving him her risqué invitation. Of course, he would want to tease her back.

"Do not mock me Ernest." She tried to keep her tone light-hearted, "You cannot deny seeing me last night."

Ernest stopped in his tracks, looking more confused than ever. Panic began to take over her. "You were there! I saw you. You told me that you would be wearing a blue flower to match my eyes and I saw you wearing that flower." Connie heard her voice begin to plead.

"I do not know who you saw, my love, but it most certainly wasn't me. I should not have been able to resist speaking to you." Upon seeing the look on her face, Ernest began to worry. "Constance, what is wrong? You've lost all colour."

"But if it was not you there last night then………. oh god………what have I done?" Connie felt as if she may faint at any moment. She closed her eyes in an attempt to calm herself when she opened them again and looked at her fiancé, she felt as though ice were running through her veins.

He knew.

"Lady Constance, tell me you did not do what I think you did." She had never heard him speak with such venom before.

Looking around her, Connie felt as though the world was caging in. In panicked tones she implored, "Please forgive me my love. I saw the flower and thought it was you to whom I gave my message."

"What message?" He snarled at her.

"An invitation to meet in a private gallery," she did her utmost to resist the tears she felt rising, "where I met with you…...him and then we…...we….." She gulped; Connie did not think she could say the words.

"You kissed a strange man thinking him to be me?"

She could lie, Connie considered it. Say it was just a kiss and have that be the end of it. The wedding was only a few weeks away so if she ended up being with child it would not come too soon.

A child.

Could she look this man who had only been kind to her in the eye and lie to him about its parentage? Could she allow another man to father his heir? And could she in good conscience keep a man from his own flesh and blood. They may not have raised her to be entirely pure, but James and Cora Wexford raised their daughter to be honest. She could not lie to this man. No matter the cost.

"I gave myself to him." The tears silently began to fall now. She did not take her eyes off him as he processed what he had just heard. His own eyes hardened, and he looked at her with complete and utter disdain. His next words were spoken slowly and harshly.

"Even had I been in attendance last night, I would have been repulsed by your behaviour." Each word cut Connie to her core. "I want a wife who can be trusted to not give in to foolish, lustful desires. A woman who carries herself with decorum. Instead, I see stood before me a trollop not worthy of my name."

She let him speak uninterrupted. Connie knew there was no point trying to protest now. "I refuse to allow this proposed marriage to go any further. Have no fear, I shall not utter a word of your deplorable actions. But you can explain to the Duke and Duchess why their daughter has ruined their name and destroyed any chance of a decent match."

He proceeded to walk away without even a word of goodbye.

Connie did not realise that she had returned home until she had closed her bedroom door behind her. Staggering to her bed, she collapsed onto it and unleashed the sobs that she had been holding back. She did not hear the knock at her door nor it opening and closing until she felt the arms envelope her.

Not knowing who it was holding her, Connie wept and wept until she felt she had no more tears left to fall. Looking up, she saw the green eyes of her beloved Duncan and, grasping once again what she had done, pleaded for forgiveness.

"Please don't hate me." She timidly uttered, "I am a fool and I have shamed us all but please don't hate me."

Worry etched onto Duncan's face, gently wiping the tears from her cheeks, he spoke softly as if to a child. "Little one, I do not think I could find a single deed you could commit and still not love you."

Connie smiled but it did not reach her eyes. Seeing that he was waiting for her to speak, she divulged the whole sordid tale.

"I suppose I shall have to be sent away; we cannot risk my shaming the family any more than I already have done."

Her brother chuckled at her as if she were a melodramatic child once again. Grasping her hands, Duncan sought to reassure her the best he could.

"Don't be silly, you are the only daughter of a duke and we are a wealthy family. Men will always be willing to marry you even if they find out you are no longer a maid. And they won't find out!" He added before she could interrupt. "But before it comes to that, we have one job to do."

Smiling half-heartedly at him, Connie queried, "And what is that dear brother." A sly grin emerged on his face.

"We are going to our stupid older brothers house and we are going to annoy him by bypassing him to find his much-maligned wife who will provide us with a list of every man at that blasted ball. And once we find him, we shall convince him to marry you."

"And how will you do that might I ask?"

"I have fists do I not?"

Chapter Five

The conversation directed towards him at brunch was incredibly stilted and the atmosphere was tense. Following the awkward meal, Xander was in the drawing room of Ainsworth House, sat in a pale green chair as he listened to Baroness Colette Philpott, the eldest daughter of the Ainsworth clan, describe her preparations for her child's arrival in the coming months.

"It was hard deciding when to leave for Kent, but Larry thought it would be more comforting to go now rather than wait for the end of the season." Colette softly touched her growing bump as she spoke, "At least I can ensure everything will be readied sooner rather than later, in case any problems occur."

Seeing her daughter bite her lip in worry over the possibility of such issues, Verity Ainsworth took her hand, "And the sooner you are settled the sooner you can send for me." Colette visibly relaxed at the touch.

Xander considered as he observed the pair that he had never seen their two profiles at the same time. If not for the trademark golden Ainsworth hair Colette possessed, as opposed to her mother's pale blonde, they could be twins. Verity did not even look old enough to be her mother. Indeed, at the age of one and forty, one could be forgiven for thinking her twenty years younger. He was shocked the day he first met her. This was the woman who had not only birthed the four lively Ainsworth's but had raised them along with an additional albeit much more even-tempered child. No one could tell.

"I'm not sure how much good that will do you though," Liam smirked, "She'll be accompanied by Eliza and Marie. That certainly will not help your nerves."

Eliza appeared decidedly put out by her brother's comment. "I will have you know that I should be a great relief to our sister." She asserted, "When I put my mind to something, I am incredibly organised and supportive."

"I have every faith Elizabeth will know exactly how to behave when the time comes."

"Are you trying to convince your children of that, My Lady, or yourself?" Xander remarked, noting how Verity almost looked up in prayer as she made her comment.

Her eldest daughter decided to answer the question for her, "Of course she shall. Besides, she knows how to behave when she is not in her own home and I will take much joy in reminding her that it is MY home we shall be in." Colette gave a rather smug look to which her sister rolled her eyes.

"I shan't be able to obtain my own home if I were taken away from a busy London season to potter about in Bloomfields." She said the name in disgust, "I'd much rather stay here in the city."

It quickly became obvious to Xander by the way she furrowed her brow that the girl was concocting ways to plot her escape from the country. As if sensing his gaze upon her, she turned to meet his. The way her eyes narrowed at him sent a clear message that she had not forgiven him for his behaviour the night before. But as unnerving as they were, it was not until they lit up and the corners of her mouth lifted that he felt a chill run down his spine.

Pursing her lips in satisfaction, Eliza suddenly took upon a wistful tone as she spoke, "Of course, in all likelihood I will not be able to accompany you, Mother. Not whilst I am needed here."

What was she up to? Whatever it was, Xander thought, there was a distinct possibility it involved him. The idea was not amusing.

"What on Earth could you mean?" Colette asked whilst their mother responded, "What could possibly more important than the birth of your first nephew."

Casually stirring her tea Eliza dodged the question, "You have no way of knowing it is a boy Mother!"

"I knew what all five of you children would be just as I knew what all my brother's and sisters' children would come out as." With an exasperated tone she added, "And you, daughter, are avoiding the question. Tell me now why you should not accompany us to Kent." Eliza opened her mouth to respond, "An honest and serious answer please or else I shall call Miss Patrick to come put you over her knee."

Eliza's mouth promptly closed as her siblings laughed at her. Beatrice Patrick had been the governess for the Ainsworth children and was infamous for her no-nonsense character. One particularly famous instance was when, at the tender age of nine, Eliza announced she would name her firstborn child after the woman and sincerely hoped it would be a boy to match Miss Patrick's frame. Eliza exaggerated that she had been unable to sit down for days as a result. Liam had privately confessed that her punishment had been the worst any of them had received but it was the result of a long line of cheeky remarks from the girl that day and the governess had lost her patience.

Eliza's announcement quickly changed the mood. Beaming, she exclaimed, "Why, someone has to be here to see to Xander's marriage of course."

Silence fell over the room as her words were processed, quickly followed by raging laughter from Verity and Colette. The rest of the company allowed the pair to let it all out. Liam and Xander exchanged serious looks as Marie suddenly found her fingernails exceptionally fascinating.

The laughter died down as the mother and daughter realised they were the only ones who found this news amusing. They soon paled at the looks on others faces.

Liam broke the silence, "I'm afraid she's being quite serious." Verity scolded her son, "Don't be silly William. Alexander and you are both three and twenty, that is no age for a man to marry. The eldest Wexford boy is a prime example of what happens when a boy marries when he is not yet a man."

"Mother, it does not matter how ol…"

Cutting her son off she continued, "Can you imagine where you would be now if we had allowed you to enter that foolish marriage you wanted when you were eighteen." That piqued the interest of everyone in the room.

Sensing her brothers' discomfort and seeming to know more to the story than everyone else, Colette sought an explanation. "Maybe you should inform us why it seems to be necessary for Xander to marry. We may be able to bring you all to your senses."

Frowning, Xander reached into the pocket of his waistcoat to retrieve the note that started the trouble. Leaning over to pass it to the Duchess, he quietly muttered, "I can only give my apologies for what you are about to hear, I should have been better."

He felt ashamed at the crestfallen look on Verity's face. The closest thing he had to a loving mother and she would be so disappointed in him. She raised her eyebrows as she read the note and turned her gaze to his as she handed it to her eldest daughter.

"Explain. Now."

"I followed the directions on the note and I…. I…..." Xander struggled to find the right words to say. Liam finished the story for him.

"The fool deflowered a young lady." Verity, Colette, and Eliza all gasped at his words. "You were there Eliza!" That remark received another collection of gasps which Xander quickly sought to rectify, "It was a different woman! Don't fret, Eliza is still a maid……I think." She smirked at that comment.

"The state of Eliza's virginity is besides the point," quickly turning to Eliza he admonished, "you better be a virgin!" Returning to the rest, "As if the deflowering were not bad enough, he doesn't even know who the chit was."

Four pairs of eyes stared at Xander in varying degrees of horror and frustration. Feeling the need to defend himself, Xander added "If I had known I would not have let it progress any further. The way she was receiving my attentions gave me the distinct impression that she was a knowledgeable woman. *I thought she was married or a widow for Christ's sake!*"

"Well, she wasn't married or a widow. The fact of the matter is you ruined a girl and if it were myself or Marie placed in the same situation, I can guarantee you would move heaven and earth to get a ring on our fingers." Xander felt a foot tall under the admonishments of Eliza. She softened her tone as she continued, "I feel horrible that I have a father, two brothers and two further honorary brothers that would fight for me. What if she doesn't have that?"

It was at this point that Marie decided to contribute to the conversation. Leaning to her cousin, she placed her hand over Eliza's, "Well she has us even if she doesn't know it." Not removing her hand, she turned to Xander, "I couldn't sleep last night so I wrote up a few lists of all the clues we have and the possible identities."

"I appear to have raised wonderful girls after all," All eyes turned to Verity as she wiped tears away, "Oh please ignore me. Marie dearest, please tell us what you think so far."

Wringing her hands together, Marie recalled her theories thus far. "Well, the note was signed with the letter 'C' which means that it is a lady known by a name beginning with the letter. As a maiden it is most likely her forename as a title would mean she was married and let us be honest what woman is known by her surname?"

Xander briefly interrupted, "She could also be known by a nickname. I have an...ahem...actress friend who is known by a 'C' name." Out of the corner of his eye he could see Liam cover his mouth to stifle a laugh. "My apologies, please go on."

Marie grew more confident as she continued, "Well, that's the name options. The room was dark but Xander believed she was wearing orange," Eliza scoffed, "however, as Eliza pointed out last night, she saw no one wearing that colour so we must surmise that she wore a similar flame toned colour. Therefore, a red or a dark yellow are our safest bets."

Quickly scanning the room for objections, she moved on. "You said she had dark hair, correct?" Xander nodded in affirmation, "Well, that means that she either has black or dark brown hair. Of course, she could have been wearing a wig, I believe a number of women did owing to the masked theme."

"Unfortunately, the same theme combined with the darkness hinders our ability to ascertain the features of her face and if she had any identifiable marks." Clearly cringing, she said, "I know I sound vulgar but owing to the relations you had, we can also uncover the shape of her figure."

Closing his eyes, Xander pinched his leg to quell the desire that suddenly surged through him at the memory of her body. "She was, um, well endowed.......in both the chest and hips. Other than that, she was generally trim." He could not meet anyone's eyes as he spoke.

"Well then. We're searching for a likely dark-haired young lady with an ample bosom who's first name probably begins with the letter 'C'." Observing the company, Marie uncharacteristically took charge, "Clearly when it comes to ladies' fashions, Eliza should aim to uncover details of the dresses worn by her fellow debs. I believe there are a great number of functions you are attending where you can discuss what outfits were worn?" Eliza nodded in assent, eyes glinting in admiration.

"Aunt Verity, you are good friends with Viscountess Coleman are you not? Therefore, it should not be hard to uncover a list of all the ladies in attendance last night, allowing us to find 'C' names." She then turned to Liam, "Cousin, you are to subtlety enquire with the members of your club if there are any brothers or fathers who are behaving in an odd manner. In my opinion men tend to be rather obvious when one of their own is in peril. Additionally, you will enjoy this, you will be appraising the bodies of the unmarried women of the ton, including the wallflowers."

Liam rubbed his hands together in glee, "Of course, men have a way of appraising women in ways that other ladies could not."

Colette shifted in her seat, "Is there anything I can do? I may be with child but surely I can help in the next few weeks before I leave."

Marie smiled, "You have an appointment with the dressmaker correct? I am sure if you drop into the conversation being particularly entranced with a colour you saw at the ball, she will reveal some information for you. Perhaps give you swatches of fabrics to compare."

"Servants love to gossip, and I will oversee sending our ones out to uncover any that may be relevant. A loss of virginity means blood stains in most cases. Owing to how it happened in this instance," she gave Xander a disconcerting look, "there will not be stains on bedsheets, but her dress and drawers should be enough evidence and the servants will know."

Sitting back in her chair, Marie only now took in the surprised looks on the faces staring at her. Defensively, she said "Just because I do not speak as much as the rest of you does not mean I am lacking in brain cells, I simply choose what I think I can contribute to."

Xander clapped his hands in admiration, "You are the most magnificent member of the entire Ainsworth clan!"

Marie beamed at him, "We are going to a large amount of fuss to preserve your honour, My Lord. A small part of me hopes that the woman you find will make you utterly miserable!"

Chapter Six

Connie was beginning to grow ever more despondent over how futile the search had become. Every function she attended gave her no clue as to the identity of her masked man and Duncan was having to reduce his efforts at his club as his searching for a man had begun resulting in "undesirable offers" he said. To his meaning, Connie could not explain.

It had been almost a month since the liaison had taken place and Connie knew that if she and Duncan were unable to make any progress soon. She would have to inform her parents. Their reaction may not be as bad as she feared, Connie considered, but she was still afraid of the look on her parents faces when she told them.

At the current moment she was promenading in the grounds of the Viscount O'Neill, whose wife was hosting a garden party. With her arm in that of her youngest brother, Connie shivered at the sense of déjà vu it imparted upon her. Her memories of that night were then disrupted by Harry.

"You know, you are going to have to tell me what is wrong with you eventually." Connie rolled her eyes at him.

"My engagement has broken, and I have become a target of gossip and you are asking me what is wrong? My dear brother, I thought you were more intelligent than that." The gossip unnerved her, for every occasion which she observed anyone looking at her and whispering to their companions, she feared that they were talking of more than just her broken engagement.

"If you are certain there is nothing more, I shall believe you, but I shan't be surprised if anything else does come about." Harry clearly did not believe her!

They passed by several friends and acquaintances, leading to Connie to wonder exactly where her brother was leading her. Looking up, her question was quickly answered as she saw the figure of Lady Eliza Ainsworth in the direction they were heading to.

Looking up at her brother, Connie could not decide what exactly the expression on his face meant. Whatever it was, it gave her pause for anything to do with a child of the Duke of Bristol would surely result in trouble.

"Lady Eliza, you are looking utterly divine today." The lady in question turned her head to the pair at Harry's words and her lips tilted in a cool smile.

"Lord Henry, fancy running into you here." She held out her hand for Harry to kiss, he eagerly dropped his sister's arm to take the offer.

"A great coincidence, I am sure. Although I do remember asking you to call me Harry, did I not?"

"Well, *Lord Henry*, I only call people by their given names when they prove themselves to be kind and respectful. You clearly are not if you are refraining from formally introducing your sister and I to one another." She gave Harry a pointed look as she spoke.

"Connie, this is Eliza. Eliza this is Connie." Harry quickly ignored his sister again. "You know I was taking a walk along The Serpentine this morning and came across an artist whose drawings I just knew you would adore. You must allow me to escort you to meet him on the morrow."

Connie had to refrain from laughing when the lady pointedly ignored Harry in favour of herself.

"Lady Constance, I must say your dress is most becoming on you. The blue is divine."

"Why thank you, Lady Elizabeth, I have to return the compliment. You do look oh so fetching."

"Please call me Eliza and I hope I have the blessing to call you Connie?" She found it intriguing how the blonde lady seemed rather keen to engage in a far more familiar friendship than was appropriate for an Ainsworth and a Wexford. The thought made Connie nervous, realising that the flirtation between the lady and her brother was more serious than they had realised.

"If you insist, Eliza. Are you here with your family this afternoon?" Connie asked.

"My sister, Colette, is around here somewhere. I imagine she is taking advantage of the fact that her condition has allowed her to indulge in the refreshments excessively without any judgement."

Connie had to laugh. "Your sister is highly intelligent in that case."

"Without a doubt," Eliza said fondly, "us women must take advantage of what we can, must we not?"

"I assure you," Harry butted in, "that when we are married, I will insist that you eat to your heart's content." Connie froze at her brother's words, but Eliza appeared to remain unperturbed.

"Are we to marry, Lord Henry? Interesting, I cannot seem to recall your proposal, I surely would have used it to practice my skills at the sympathetic refusal."

"Perhaps that is because you never seem to answer my questions at all." He turned to Connie to address her. "Sister dear, I made a particular request of this lady not a moment ago, do you remember if she answered me? For I cannot find the memory whatsoever."

"Do not bring me into this, Harry." Connie responded.

"Why should I accept your request, Lord Henry?" Eliza dispassionately asked. "You have given me no reason to."

"If my very purpose for drawing breath not reason enough?" Both women's eyebrows raised, wondering where Harry was leading them.

"If my words held the power of life and death, I would certainly not be wasting my life away on the marriage market." The lady was clearly not giving in to the bait.

"In two weeks, I shall be off to fight, Eliza, if all I shall be left with is your rejection, I shall have no choice but to throw myself into the path of the nearest enemy rifle."

"Oh, how deliciously morbid." Eliza smirked.

"In that case, Eliza, please turn my brother down." Connie played along. "He is too much of a nuisance as it is, and I shan't miss him if he's gone."

"Connie that argument is a total lie, and you know it." Harry retorted. "You would be beside yourself without me. I am your favourite brother, after all."

"Anyone in the family would tell you that Duncan is my favourite brother, just do not tell him that." Connie replied.

Eliza interrupted the pair with a delighted grin on her face. "I am afraid that my own favourite brother has decided to announce his return to London by arriving here now. If you will both excuse me, I must greet him."

The lady turned to Connie, taking her hand in hers. "It was lovely to have met you, Connie. I do hope we shall see each other again soon."

Rather than bid her goodbyes to Harry, she opted to look his body up and down in mock disgust before leaving.

Harry quickly grasped her arm to stop her. "You will meet me tomorrow, will you not?" Connie almost gasped at the sheer seriousness in her brother's eyes at the question. This was far more worrisome than she had supposed.

A brief look of tenderness crossed the lady's features before she masked her expression. "I suppose if your life depends on it, my conscience could not allow me to refuse."

Gently extracting herself from Harry's grasp, Eliza left the pair to return to her siblings. For several moments, Harry did not seem to be aware of anything but the woman who he remained watching.

With a troubled look on her face, Connie soothingly rubbed his arm, placing her hand in his elbow before speaking. "Be careful there brother. You may joke but we both know there's more harm than good down that path."

Connie stood staring at the oak door of her father's office for several minutes, struggling to find the courage to lift her hand and knock. She knew that the moment she did so, there was no going back, and her father would never look at her the same again.

"My, my, I have not seen that expression since you were four and ten."

Connie rapidly blinked before turning her head to her left and seeing her mother stood beside her, eyebrows raised and worry in her eyes. The older woman put her arm around her daughter and squeezed her shoulders.

"Whatever it is, my sweet, I am certain it is not as bad as you think."

"I should think you are grossly overestimating how good I am." Connie heard her voice crack as tears filled her eyes.

"Come on dearest, the sooner we get this over with, the sooner your father and I can set it right. Whatever it may be."

Opening the door, Cora ushered her daughter into the room where her husband sat at his desk mulling over an atlas. James Wexford, Duke of Gloucester looked up, happy to see his favourite women. His joy quickly dissipated, however, when he saw the anguish in his daughter's eyes.

As Connie was placed in one of the chairs positioned before the desk, her mother sitting beside her, she looked up to see her father had moved around the desk to perch against it before her.

Hands shaking, her head darted back and forth between each parent as Connie felt all the emotions of the past few weeks rise from the pit of her stomach before bubbling over and she revealed all of the sorry tale to the pair.

Once she had finished speaking, Connie's head fell and she fixed her stare upon her hands, unwavering. She did not know what she dreaded more, the disappointment or the chastisement.

A soft hand came to rest under her chin before it gently nudged her to lift her head. Looking up, she saw her mother had moved to kneel before her.

"Oh, my sweet, I am so sorry you have had to go through this all alone."

Confusion crossed Connie's features at her mother's words. *Why was she being so kind?*

"Are you not furious with me?" she asked. "I gave my maidenhood to a man who I did not know, whilst engaged to another man."

"If I heard correctly, Constance," her father said, "you were under the impression the man in question was your fiancé. It does explain why Fawcett ending things so abruptly." He rubbed his hand over his chin as he drifted into his thoughts.

"Things are not as dire as you may think, Connie." Her eyes drifted back to her mother. "You are the daughter of a duke, after all. I can safely say in this world that men will be quick to abandon their morals when wealth and power are offered. So, you do not need to fear on that account."

"Perhaps," the duke absentmindedly said before straightening his back and speaking up, "there does remain, however, one rather important question. A question I had never expected to ask."

Connie unconsciously chewed the side of her mouth as she anticipated her father's question.

"When did you last bleed, Constance?" The tears began to rise again as he spoke. Taking a deep breath, Connie spluttered out that it had been "before the ball."

Her father groaned and began to pace whilst his wife moved to take a seat again, taking Connie's hand to hold.

After several minutes of tenseness, with the only sound being that of her father's footprints as he strode back and forth, Cora entreated her husband.

"James, love, I do not think your pacing is doing any good for our daughter's nerves……. or my own for that matter!"

The duke stilled then returned to his place before the desk, where he crossed his arms and looked down at the women.

"Given the circumstances, I believe there are two possibilities I can put forth." Connie took a breath as she nodded at her father to continue.

"There are several older gentlemen with titles who have no direct heirs to pass their titles to. They would be accepting of you and a child, and you would be left a young, titled widow with the freedom to choose whomever you wish for your next husband."

"Well, that is morbid." She dryly stated, prompting a pointed look from both parents.

"Alternatively, you can marry a younger man not in possession of a title who will be accepting of your situation as it will provide him with wealth and ties to a powerful family. You are, however, unlikely in this scenario to have a second husband."

"So those are my choices?" Connie asked. "Either an old lech or a young social climber?" She was tempted to reject both choices outright.

"Sweetness, you are an unmarried woman who may be carrying a stranger's child. It may not be fair, but you have limited yourself with your actions."

Connie winced at her mother's words. Much to her regret, she had to admit they were true. There was, however, a third option that had not been mentioned as of yet.

"And the father?" she prompted. "Does he not deserve to be considered?" James laughed in response.

"A man who deflowers young maidens at society functions? Forgive me if I do not hold my breath over his making an appearance."

Thoughts whizzed through Connie's mind as she considered the best way to appease both her father and her conscience, which would not allow her to throw herself into marriage without at least trying further to find her masked man.

An idea came to her mind, and she prayed that her father would agree to it. "What if I put forward a compromise, Papa?" She crossed her fingers, hidden in the folds of her dress as her father's eyebrows lifted in curiosity.

"I will agree to marry an older, titled man that you put forth on the condition that should the father be found at any point before the wedding, I be allowed to marry him instead."

"Providing he would be willing?" Cora questioned, to which Connie nodded in assent.

"Hmmm," the duke pursed his lips in consideration, "and what of the scandal? It would be fodder for the entire ton."

"When they are whispering behind our backs, they will be sure to say how it is not surprising that a young lady would rather marry a man closer to her own age than the man who will be jilted." She countered.

Connie waited with bated breath for her father to decide. He shared a look with her mother, seeming to ask her permission, before he muttered that he agreed to her terms.

Smiling victoriously, Connie felt as though a weight had been lifted off her shoulders. Now with both a deadline and a new motivation, she found herself more determined than ever to find her masked man and convince him to wed.

Bidding her parents goodnight, both thanking and apologising to them, she left the study and retired for the night. For the first night in almost a month, Connie was able to fall asleep the moment her head hit the pillow.

Chapter Seven

Xander watched the amber liquid swirl around his glass as he half-listened to Calvert describing the developments of a steam-powered locomotive that they had made an investment in the previous year.

"I believe Stephenson is progressing well, but it will be many years before we see a profit." "That is no matter," Liam responded, "as long as people keep reading, our printing press' will support us fine."

More than fine, thought Xander, the amount of money their investments were making ensured that even if this venture were not a success, they would be able to live comfortably for several lifetimes.

He remained concerned as to how he would find his mysterious maiden, well former maiden. It seemed as though they had exhausted all avenues. Each of them had compiled a list of suspects but unfortunately not one name appeared on everyone's list. Added to this was the fact that there appeared to be no gossip whatsoever amongst the ton or the servants regarding it.

The frustration was killing him. It was even taking over his sleep. Every night he had the same dream: He was in the portrait gallery with his lady in his arms. The pair were making love and just when he was on the verge of release she ran away. He chased after her and, just as he was about to grab her, he woke up sweating, his cock stiff and a sense of desperation overtaking him.

Every. Single. Night.

He was brought out of his musings when he noticed that no one was speaking. Looking up, he saw Calvert, Liam and Freddie all staring at him. Sitting up in his chair, he coughed out an apology. "Sorry, I was just thinking about......ahem......"

"Former virgins?" Freddie grinned. All three men laughed as Xander felt the heat rise in his face. He attempted to turn the subject back to their investments, but his friends would not relent so easily.

"You really must let it go Sutton," said Liam, "we cannot seem to find the girl anywhere. As much as I am enjoying feasting my eyes over the ladies of the ton there does not seem to be any point in continuing."

Having only just returned to London, Freddie was determined not to miss out on the fun, "No, we cannot give up now. I refuse to let you have all the fun without me." He slouched on the chaise as he continued, "There must be some line of investigation you haven't followed."

"No point in trying Fred," Calvert responded, "the chit has vanished into thin air. In fact, I believe she may be off with the fairies or unicorns or other such imaginary creatures. I am not too sure I believe she is real."

The whiskey felt like fire as he emptied the contents of the glass down his throat. "She's real all right." *I can still taste her* "If I must go to every blasted ball in this frivolous town I shall but I will find her!"

Nodding his head in contemplation, Freddie mused, "I'll wager she's a spinster." Liam choked on his drink at his brother's words. "Consider it, you have all been looking at the young ladies but for all we know she's a thirty-year-old bore who is firmly on the shelf. Perhaps you should be looking for an old woman instead?" Freddie beamed as his words took effect.

Staring bemused at his brother, Liam uttered in disbelief, "Spoken like a true seventeen-year-old." Seemingly determined to fully put down his kin, he continued, "Speaking of virginity, have you lost yours yet? Or shall I offer once again to introduce you to some ladies to teach you a thing or two?"

Dropping his face, Freddie mumbled something under his breath about there being "no need now." Before anyone had the chance to respond, Eliza burst through the door looking remarkably like the cat who got the cream.

"Oh, am I interrupting something?" Unceremoniously throwing herself down next to her youngest brother, she observed the company. "Please do not stop on my account, I am not as delicate as father would have you believe."

A flicker of amusement on his face, Calvert opened his mouth to respond before Freddie blurted out "Any of you say anything and I shall castrate you in your sleep."

Once again, Liam choked on his drink at his brother's words. Xander thumped him on the back several times until his coughing was under control. "And how, may I ask, will you accomplish that?" He questioned, wiping tears from his face.

"I have my ways," Freddie responded, "I have to find some way to get my hands on the Duchy anyway. If you behave well, brother, I shall allow you to grow old as well. If not, then......." Grinning menacingly, he crossed a finger over his throat.

"This is why I'm glad I am an only child." Calvert chortled.

"Count yourself lucky," Xander said to Liam, "I have two brothers to deal with."

"I saw one of them on my walk today actually." Eliza announced, "Richard I think it was or it could have been Paul. How can you tell who's who?"

"You can't, they're identical twins."

"How unnerving was that to grow up with?" Calvert asked.

"It wasn't so bad. The only problems were when they tried to confuse you when one of them was in trouble. I remember on one occasion when I was seven Paul decided to pour jam into my shoes." He shivered as he remembered the feeling when he put them on his feet. "He was adamant it was Dickie who had done the deed in spite of the fact that he still had the substance on his hands."

Eliza's mouth contorted in distaste at the thought, "Charming. Well, whichever one it was I saw he appeared to be sleeping on a bench. We only knew he was alive by how the spotted handkerchief lying across his face lifted whenever he breathed. That and the snoring was rather loud."

Running his hand through his hair in resignation Xander identified his brother, "Dickie most likely, probably was in his cups until the sun rose as usual. It's a miracle that boy isn't dead yet."

Eliza nudged her brother, "Stay away from him Freddie, it may be catching."

Looking incredulously at his sister, Freddie remarked, "You don't honestly believe that men get intoxicated like they catch a cold, do you?" Putting his hand on her shoulder, he pressed further, "I need to hear you say you know that. I refuse to allow a sister of mine to be that naïve."

Shooing his hand away, Eliza locked eyes with Xander. "Sutton dear, I need you to repeat exactly what I am about to say, do you understand?"

He was wary of the sudden change in conversation. "What are you up to?"

"You won't find out unless you repeat after me. Are you ready?"

Curious as to what she was about to say, Xander leaned back in his chair and nodded.

Grinning, Eliza began. "Lady Elizabeth, I am so grateful to have you in my life."

Rolling his eyes, he repeated.

"It truly devastates me that I shall never be able to make you my bride."

Calvert attempted to stifle his laughter with his hand.

"In fact, if your brothers were not here now, I would hold you in my arms and kiss you firmly on the mouth in gratitude."

"ELIZA!" She shushed her brother and looked expectantly at Xander.

"I'm not going to continue until you repeat what I said."

Xander raised his eyebrows in amusement, "I wouldn't kiss you firmly, you little minx, I would kiss you thoroughly."

The way her cheeks went pink was well worth the slap Liam administered to the back of his head. Waving his hand, Xander beckoned her to continue.

"And I shall be forever in your debt......."

"And I shall be forever in your debt."

"Because you have done the impossible and found my mystery maiden."

All four men gaped in shock following her words. Then Xander promptly stood up, walked over to Eliza, grasped her by the arms, hauled her to her feet and kissed her. Firmly.

Releasing her, Xander turned to Liam who had approached to free his sister and promptly kissed him too. "Your sister is bloody marvellous!"

The two elder Ainsworth siblings were stood still in shock, Freddie had jumped behind the sofa in an attempt to ensure he himself would not become acquainted with Xander's mouth whilst Calvert casually strolled to the whiskey decanter and refilled Xander's glass. Handing it back to him, he remarked, "It would be a shame if, after all the weeks of lusting after the girl, you lost your balls now by attempted *that* with me."

Downing his glass, Xander made two deep breaths and turned to the pair still stood like statues, "My apologies, got a bit carried away there."

As he returned to his seat, the pair seemed to finally come back to life. Eliza fell back onto the chaise in hysterical laughter whilst Liam staggered back to his seat in a stupor. Picking the decanter up, he refilled his glass, appeared to take a moment of consideration, and promptly drank straight from the decanter. Licking his lips after taking several swigs, he pointed his finger towards Xander, "Never again, you hear me?" Xander nodded, still beaming from the news.

Observing Freddie peering from behind the chaise, Xander called to him, "Have no fear Freddie, I've recovered from my brief moment of hysteria."

Reluctantly, Freddie returned to his seat, although he sat in preparation to make a run for it if he needed.

Wiping the tears from her eyes, Eliza let out a few more mute laughs before resuming her story. "Oh gosh, that is the most fun I have had all week! Now, would you like the good news or the bad news?"

"Oh god, I'm too late, aren't I?" Xander said ruefully.

"No, no. Do not worry on that account, she is very much available." Appearing to consider her words carefully, a rarity for Eliza, she continued, "It is not so much those details which are a worry. I have spoken to her before and found her quite pleasant. The problem is that she is…...she's a…….."

Impatient, Liam barked, "For god's sake Eliza, who the bloody well is she?"

"Constance Wexford."

The first time Eliza had silenced the room it was in shock and awe. On this occasion, it was in horror. The atmosphere became very sombre indeed.

Slowly leaning forward, Xander spoke, "Eliza, are you absolutely certain that's who she is?"

This was the most serious she had ever appeared to him, "Well, I am not entirely sure, but everything matches up and her engagement ended just after the ball. It was rather a surprise so something rather big must have happened to end it."

She was engaged? That would explain why she wanted to meet with him before it was too late, Xander mused, but why on earth would Constance Wexford want anything to do with him? He has never even met the girl! Well, he may have now.

Taking his head in his hands he pushed Eliza further, "How have you come to this conclusion? We have to be absolutely sure."

"Harry and I were discussing the ball and I thought that maybe…."

"*Harry and I were discussing the ball?* Why were you having discussions with Harry Wexford?" Liam interjected.

"We could not very well go on a walk together in silence, now could we? Now, where was I?"

The sound of movement caused Xander to lift his head. Liam was standing over his sister with his hands on his hips. "Why were you on a walk with Harry Wexford? And why is he just 'Harry' to you? I told you to stay away from the boy."

Rolling her eyes, Eliza responded, "To stop him from dying. Now regarding Constance...."

"To stop him from dying? That does not even make sense. I told you to stay away from him and as your older brother and the future head of this family I expect you to listen to me!"

"Oh, for Christ's sake Liam shut up!" Eliza burst out, "Unlike you I do not judge people based on their surnames and I most certainly do not refrain from taking an innocent walk with a young, attractive and eligible man if I should desire to. Furthermore, if you knew anything about Harry you would know that he has joined the army and will be leaving for the continent soon enough therefore nothing will come of this flirtation. Now, kindly take a seat and allow me to explain to Lord Sutton how I have come to reach the conclusion I have reached. And do remain in silence until you have something of actual consequence to say."

The pair locked eyes in an unspoken argument which Liam appeared to lose. His face devoid of any emotion, he promptly resumed his seat and loudly munched on a biscuit in his only form of protest.

Turning back to Xander, Eliza resumed, "As I was
saying before I was RUDELY interrupted, I was walking with
Harry when the topic of conversation turned to the ball. I
asked him what the reactions of his family were to our
acquaintanceship beginning." Furrowing her eyebrows, she
continued, "It struck me as he was speaking that Lady
Constance had the attributes which we were trying to find so I
told him I could not recall seeing her and enquired as to what
she was wearing. Just like a typical man he struggled to
remember so I asked him if she wore red to which he was able
to recall her wearing yellow."

"Yellow dress, black hair, rather full in, ahem, certain
areas, a name beginning with 'C' and an engagement that
came to an abrupt halt. To be frank no one else quite fits the
bill."

Xander considered all she had said. It just did not
make sense. As to her looks he could not say, unable to recall
having ever laid eyes on the girl at all. He would need to see
her in person, but the entire case bemused him.

"Why would she want me though? She specifically put
that note in my hand."

Calvert rubbed his hand over his chin, "Fawcett
wasn't it? The man she was engaged to?" Eliza nodded in
assent. "The man's a frightful bore, so self-righteous. Maybe
she wanted some excitement before her wedding, and it
backfired on her? Not too surprising she would pick you.
Ladies have always been keen where you're concerned, and

you bear enough of a passing resemblance for there to not be any questions should any spawn emerge."

"It doesn't matter anyway," Liam announced, "You're not going to marry the girl after all."

Turning to his friend, Xander enquired "Why the devil not? I ruined her; it is only fair that I take responsibility."

"She's a Wexford! Do you honestly think she would allow you to maintain an association with our family?" Liam sighed, "God knows why but the entire lot of them despise us."

"Not all of them." Eliza mumbled.

Taking his sisters hand, Freddie gently spoke, "El, just because he's willing to flirt with you does not mean he would allow himself to marry you. Like his entire family that boy is a snake and the sooner you realise it the better!"

"Good god it cannot honestly be that bad." Uttered an exasperated Calvert, "What could you have honestly done to cause that kind of animosity?"

Raising his hands in frustration, Liam said, "Nothing at all! The families were hostile after a land dispute but that was seventy-five years ago. I have tried to reach out to Matthew Wexford several times but he and the rest of them act as cold as ever. And now it seems they're willing to use Eliza as a pawn."

"In any case," Freddie said, "the girl is a daughter of a Duke, a wealthy one at that. If she finds herself in a situation then they will buy her a husband and Sutton doesn't have to worry."

The thought of another man having her made Xander's blood run cold. "I am marrying her." He spat the words out.

Ignoring him, Eliza berated her brother, "Freddie, I'm surprised at you! Are you not always saying we should be the bigger people? Why should we now ask Xander to be the worst kind of rake?"

"Wexford." Freddie shrugged as if that should answer all her questions. It did appear out of character for the boy but that was not something to be investigated for the moment.

Commanding everyone's attention, Xander stood to announce, "There is no point in having this little debate. If Lady Constance is the lady who we have been searching for then she will be my wife. There is nothing else to say on the matter."

As he turned to Eliza to decide their next step, her being his only ally in the room, Calvert leant back in his chair and folded his arms. Smiling, he said aloud to no one in particular, "Why anyone should buy tickets to the theatre when the Ainsworth's provide a show for free, I will never know."

Chapter Eight

Connie had no idea when she woke that Thursday morning just how thoroughly her life would change. She mulled over her options as Letitia helped her into a pale green morning dress and said a silent prayer of thanks that she had no plans for the day and so could attempt to relax her brain. Although she was not quite sure she would be able to after the conversation she and her Papa had had the previous night.

For the second evening in a row, Connie had entered her father's study, although this time by his invitation. James Wexford had sat her down and highlighted the best suitors for her at the current time.

Unfortunately for Constance, he recommended she aim for either Baron Kingston or Sir Alfred Chatsworth. Both gentlemen were several years older than her father and possessed extraordinarily little charm although they made up for that in girth. These factors combined with the lack of suitable heir meant that they would both be willing to claim a child not theirs and they were unlikely to live much longer. Thus, Connie would be left a young widow with the freedom to marry whomever she desired.

After breakfast Connie opted to sit in the garden, it being a particularly pleasant day, and compose a letter to her cousin Anne, who had recently been widowed, leaving her with two stepdaughters and an infant son to contend with.

Once the letter was finished, she set it aside on the bench as she stood to sniff the white roses that grew in the centre of the garden. Inhaling the sweet scent of the flower, Connie closed her eyes and lifted her head to the sun, basking in its warmth.

Ever since she was a small child, Connie had always felt that being in the garden, surrounded by peace and the soft sounds of nature, was the closest thing she had felt to heaven. Feeling the most hopeful she had been in the past month, Connie whispered a small prayer, somehow knowing that someone was listening.

"Please find him for me and oh please let him be wonderful. We need him home, with us!" As Connie slowly opened her eyes, she noticed that, unconsciously, she had rested her hand upon her abdomen. Even though it would take at least another month to confirm it and even longer for it to be visible, somehow in that moment Connie knew that she was with child and suddenly she felt a little less alone.

Smiling to herself, Connie retrieved her writing tools and slowly strode back to the house. Entering the doors to the morning room, Connie was jolted back to reality by the sight of Harry staring at a young lady who had her back to him. A golden-haired lady who appeared to be shaking.

"Lady Elizabeth?" Connie questioned, although who else would it be with Harry.

The pair both jumped and turned to her. Eliza smiled warmly and stepped forward to take both of Connie's hands.

"Lady Constance, I do hope you will forgive the intrusion, but I am afraid there were matters here that needed my attention urgently."

The shock of having an Ainsworth dare to enter a Wexford home slowly wore off Connie and she suddenly became conscious of her appearance. Her dress was creased from how she was seated in the garden, her shoes most likely muddy from the flowerbed, the rosy cheeks from being sat in the sun for far too long and her hair flowing in soft curls down her back was most improper to meet anyone in society. Connie was not sure her family should even see her with her hair down.

Even worse, Connie did not think Eliza Ainsworth could not look more proper or beautiful in that moment. Hair perfectly coiffed and pinned beneath her blue bonnet, which naturally matched her walking dress and gloves. Observing how unblemished her white shoes were, it was also clear the elegant lady had not been traipsing anywhere in an unladylike fashion, especially not rose bushes.

Returning her gaze to Eliza's face, Connie saw the expectant expression and quickly sought to return to her manners.

"Do not feel as if you are intruding My Lady, you are most welcome of course although," she glanced at Harry, "I am not sure if your urgent matter is altogether proper."

Laughing, Eliza squeezed her hands. "I think you and I would both agree that Harry here is most certainly not important enough to be an urgent matter and did I not ask you to call me Eliza when we met? I feel calling each other 'My Lady' is far too formal for the conversation we are to have. May I call you Connie?"

Nodding in assent, Connie became even more perplexed as to why Eliza was paying them a visit. Aside from Harry's flirtations the Wexford's made sure to keep a wide berth from the Ainsworths and would not willingly give them cause to come into their home.

"Please take a seat, I shall call for some tea and biscuits." Going to the door, Connie saw that several maids and their butler, Jennings, were lurking about in the hallway. Rolling her eyes as they quickly scattered, Connie relayed the orders to Jennings. Returning to the room, she observed that, whilst Eliza had settled herself into one of the chaises and removed her bonnet, Harry still stood in the centre of the room, still staring at the spot Eliza had stood.

Shoving her brother into action, Connie took a seat on the opposite chaise and noted that, as he would, Harry had opted to sit besides their guest. Although he still had yet to say a word.

Turning to the lady in question, Connie cut straight to the point. "What is the urgent matter that has brought you here Eliza? I am sure you know as well as I that both of our families will be most unhappy about this visit."

Wringing her gloved hands together, Eliza appeared nervous as she spoke. "To be altogether quite honest, I do not think I can go about this without appearing to be rather crass." Connie furrowed her brows in confusion.

"You see, it is a rather sensitive matter and although I am quite sure I have reached the correct conclusion, the risk of getting it wrong is rather offensive."

Perplexed, Connie implored, "I'm sure whatever it is you have to say, we will be neither shocked nor offended." Smiling, she continued, "After all, our families are taught to believe the worst of one another so I am sure any offence taken will be brushed away as typical Ainsworth behaviour."

This did not appear to sooth Eliza's nerves. "Well, you see, it's that I have....... I mean to say that you have....... oh, to hell with it, did you or did you not engage in a secret tryst at the Coleman ball last month?"

Connie felt a chill wash over her and felt she may possibly empty the entire contents of her stomach onto the floor. Staring in horror at the lady sat across from her, Connie could see that her reaction was all Eliza Ainsworth needed to confirm her belief.

It was at this moment that Harry was brought out of his stupor. Hoping to reduce the risk of her actions getting out, pointless as that now appeared to be, Connie had ensured that the only ones who knew what happened were her parents and Duncan. Naturally because of this, Harry was quick to jump to his sister's defence.

Grabbing Eliza's arm, Harry practically spat his words out at the girl. "How dare you have the nerve to accuse my sister of such a thing!" Ignoring Eliza's beseeches to let her go, he continued. "My sister is a good and honourable woman, and I will not have a woman like you ruin her reputation."

As Connie stood to attempt to assist the damsel from her brother, a deep voice rang through the room causing goosebumps to erupt all over Connie's body.

"Unhand the lady now sir or I shall remove your hands myself!"

All three heads rapidly turned to the owner of the voice and Connie gasped in shock. Recognising the jet-black hair and blue eyes so dark they were almost black. Her prayer had been answered. The masked man had found her. Falling back onto the seat in shock, Connie could scarcely believe he was here.

"Xander darling, you really do have the most perfect timing you know!" Eliza's voice did little to recover Connie. It did seem to bring Harry out of his rage though.

"Who are you sir, why are you in my house and why is she calling you darling?" He asked, with each question seemingly more urgent than the last.

The stranger bowed his head as he identified himself. "Alexander Chalmers, Earl of Sutton at your service sir." He said, "I was told I may have ruined a lady here and this one insisted I give the lady justice." Turning his eyes to Connie, "I see Eliza was correct in her assumptions."

Sparks of awareness jolted through Connie as their eyes met. The memories of their meeting rang through her head and she could not help biting her lip as she remembered the way his hands had pleasured her.

"Oh god Connie, please tell me you didn't."

Turning to her brother, she could not help but feel ashamed. "I am afraid I did" muttered Connie. Running his hands through his hair, Harry went pale.

"If it's any help, I resolved to marry her as soon as I realised what I had done," the Earl said, "it just took a while to work out exactly which girl I had done it to."

"If it is any help, Harry dear," Eliza contributed, "it was during our walk yesterday that I realised that Connie was the young lady we had been searching for. So, if it mollifies your ego, we can give you the credit for saving your sister from scandal and making her a countess." Patting Harry on the knee in an improper but mocking fashion, Eliza gestured to the Earl. "Please take a seat next to your betrothed, My Lord, I am sure you will want to be officially introduced."

Slowly walking towards her, Connie had the distinct impression that this man was like a panther stalking towards his prey and she the prey. Willing herself to have some semblance of sense in this conversation, Connie took a deep breath and held out her hand to the man as he took his seat.

"Lady Constance Wexford, at your service sir."

He took her hand in his and brought it to his lips for the lightest of kisses. Connie blushed as the memory of his lips on hers crept over her and from the way his eyes ran over her body, she knew he was remembering it as well. Although it was other places he may be remembering his lips being.

"Please, call me Xander." He released her hand, "My apologies for not being here sooner, Constance, I am afraid you were a bit lacking in the identity department initially."

Connie softly laughed at his words. She did not know there even was an Earl of Sutton so how would he know who she was.

"Oh, for the love of god will someone please tell me what is going on? And why I am the only one in the room who knows nothing?"

Luckily for Connie, it was at that moment that a maid arrived with the tea tray and was setting it down for the group. Even more so, Eliza decided to relieve Connie of having to inform her brother of what exactly had happened.

"Your sister has waited long enough to have her conversation so we shall leave her to it, and I shall tell you instead. After you pour me a cup of tea that is."

The pair promptly forgot about Connie and Xander as they bickered over who should pour who the tea.

Xander lightly chuckled as he observed the pair, allowing Connie the chance to observe his appearance for the first time. When they had met his mask covered most of his face and there was little light to see what was not covered. Now in the light of day, she saw how defined his jawline and cheekbones were and how thick his hair was. She did not need to look down his body to know what it was like. Far too often had her mind drifted to when it was pressed up against her and she felt the firmness of him. Instead, she noticed his suit. It was simple, black with a blue waistcoat and a white shirt a cravat but the way it fitted his body and the fine materials the comprised it gave her the distinct impression that he was well able to look after himself and took pride in his appearance. Both of which presented a positive future for Connie.

Raising her eyes back to his face, Connie saw that he had turned back to her and between his smirk and the tilt of his brow told her he knew she was remembering her tryst.

Clearing his throat, he began, "Constance, before we say anything I want to reassure you that you have no fears where I am concerned. I intend to make you my wife and right the wrong I have done you. In fact, I have an appointment to procure a special license this afternoon."

Connie felt her jaw drop at that last sentence. She began to panic.

"A special license?" She said, "But that means that we would be married within the week. I need more time! There are so many things to do, and my mama shall wish to...."

"Is there a chance you are carrying my child?" He interrupted, laying his hand on hers. Looking down at their hands, she nodded.

"Then it is best for propriety's sake that I obtain the license and wed you now." Lifting her chin with his finger, Connie looked into his intense gaze. "I am sorry for what I have done. I promise that if I had known you were a maid and engaged to another man, I would not have behaved as I had."

Connie was touched by his sincerity and began to feel optimistic about marrying him. Wishing to absolve him of his guilt, Connie responded, "There is no need to apologise. You would not have been in that gallery if I had not passed you that note. Besides, if the note had gone to its intended recipient, I feel my status would not be entirely too different to what it is now."

Xander stiffened at her words. As he began to comprehend the meaning of them a sense of revulsion washed through him and everything changed.

The second he saw her as he entered the room, he knew she was the one he had been looking for. Her body had been imprinted onto him in that one brief tryst and seeing it before him once again had filled him with lust.

All he wanted to do was drag her to the nearest surface and bury himself inside her. He was glad he made the decision to obtain a special licence as it meant less of a wait before he could take her to his bed and keep her there.

But now the lust was all gone. It had been replaced with complete and utter disgust as one key detail was brought to the fore.

She never wanted him.

It all made sense now. He had racked his brain all night trying to discern why Lady Constance Wexford, a girl he had never met and barely even heard of, would wish to have a rendezvous with a man who was practically a member of a rival clan.

How horrifying it must be for her! He would not blame her if she hated him, he felt enough hate for himself in this moment. He could scarcely imagine how violated she must have felt.

After all, she left that room believing she had been with another man, most likely the fiancé, and then learnt not long after that it was not only an entirely different man but one whom she did not know.

Was she attending society functions in fear of being cornered and molested by the same stranger? She was a young, innocent girl and he had ruined her.   All the guilt he felt now multiplied.

Standing suddenly, he nodded in her direction, not quite able to meet her eyes. "Lady Constance, I will obtain the license and shall send word when the date is set. I shall ensure you will want for nothing. Now if you will excuse me, I have matters to attend to."

Not looking back, Xander promptly walked out and enquired with the butler as to when he would be able to speak with the Duke. Upon agreeing to return at a later time for a meeting, he was led to the front door.

Feeling eyes on his back, Xander turned and saw that Constance had followed him. Wide-eyed and biting her lip, she stared at him. A surge of lust took over him. He desperately wanted to run his hands through the loose hair and bite her lip himself.

Instead, he nodded and left the house. The next time he would see her would be four days later, walking down the aisle to become his wife.

Chapter Nine

It was a good thing that they had decided to have a small wedding, Xander mused. When news of their nuptials broke across the ton, every single person had a comment to make in the way of speculating as to how the unexpected match had come about. Needless to say, that if the wedding had not been intimate then the entire ton would have shown up and been privy to the foul mood of the groom.

As he stood at the altar, waiting for the wedding to begin, he observed the attendants and decided he had never seen a more tense crowd in his life. On his side of the church sat his immediate family: his mother and two brothers, in addition to the entire Ainsworth clan with Liam stood by his side as his best man.

Exchanging hostile looks with them from the other side were the Wexfords sans Connie and her father, who were expected at any moment. Xander started at the sight of Duncan Wexford directing to him a murderous gaze whilst cracking his knuckles. This could possibly go down as the most miserable affair in the history of England!

"Such a pleasant lot, your new family, are they not?" Liam murmured to him. Looking him in the eye, Xander said "Let us just get this over with. The sooner this intolerable ceremony is conducted the sooner we can get in our cups."

Raising his eyebrows in amusement at the comment, Liam grinned as he looked around. His gaze suddenly halted.

"Get ready, time to play pretend."

Following his line of vision, Xander turned to look towards the doors of the church, where Connie and her father now stood. As if it knew how his heart leapt in his chest, the bridal march began, and the pair began to walk up the aisle.

Connie wore a silver dress of silk and carried a bouquet of wildflowers in her gloved hands. Her hair was pinned into a loose chignon with free tendrils of her raven hair framing her face. It struck Xander that she could elicit such a reaction from him when this was only their third meeting.

He knew practically nothing about the girl. A million questions soared through his mind. Did she like to read? What was her favourite food? Did she enjoy the theatre? He had never heard her truly laugh; he did not know her desires in life. Even the memory of her body imprinted on his was just a peek into her true being. He wanted so much to learn more about her but there was one thing he knew without a doubt. She did not want him and never had.

She would not meet his eyes through the whole ceremony. He could not help but feel guilty. She was being forced to marry a man she never wished to wed. The poor girl must be terrified! She knew as little about him as he knew of her. As far as he knew, Connie believed she was entering into marriage with a cruel rake who took advantage of innocent girls at society affairs.

This was easily the worst part. There was nothing he desired more than to carry her to his bed and spend an eternity burning himself onto her skin. Teaching her how to please him and only him. But he could not do this to her. As painful as it would be, he would keep his distance and hopefully, in time, she would warm to him and would willingly invite him to her bed.

It was only upon the declaration that they were man and wife that her eyes finally met his. The look that met his was queer, her eyes did not appear to be fearful, but he could not name the emotion that he saw in them.

Realising that he had been given leave to kiss his bride, his eyes drifted down to her lips and the memory stirred of how they felt against his. Lust poured through him as he imagined those soft, plump lips kissing every inch of him.

Taking a deep breath, Xander leaned in and met her mouth in the faintest of kisses. He neither wished to scare her with his intensity nor incur any further wrath from her family than necessary.

Taking her hand, he placed it in the crook of his arm and walked them to the front of the church. Taking in the congregation, he saw that the service had done little to lift people's spirits.

After they exited the church, Xander ushered his new bride into his carriage which would escort them immediately to his Mayfair house. He and his new father-in-law had mutually agreed that it would be best to forgo the wedding breakfast and not force the families to have to endure one another's company any longer than necessary.

The silence was palpable as they both stared out of the windows of the carriage. Xander had no clue as to how to begin a conversation with his wife. Stealing a glance, he observed she was biting her lip and wringing her hands, no doubt in fear of what lay ahead once they reached her new home.

Clearing his throat, which made her start, Xander made the most awkward attempt of small talk in his life.

"The ceremony was rather charming, was it not?" Her eyes briefly darted to his before nodding in agreement. Her smile was obviously strained.

"And the flowers were most lovely." Once again, she nodded. This was going to be a struggle.

"Of course, the weather is perfect for a wedding day." A small squeak came from her throat in agreement.

"My highlight was most definitely how miserable every person in attendance was." Her sudden burst of laughter stilled by her hand covering her mouth. Xander smiled to himself at having obtained a reaction other than terror out of her.

As he opened his mouth to continue, the carriage jerked to a halt and Xander silently cursed as he stepped out onto the street. Turning back to assist her out of the carriage, he then led her up the steps and into the house, where the servants were all stood in line awaiting introductions.

The pair slowly walked along the line as he introduced her to various servants as the new mistress of the house. When they came to the end of the line, however, Xander's brows furrowed in confusion at the unfamiliar face before him.

Seeing his confusion, Connie softly squeezed his arm as she spoke, "I hope you do not mind but I requested that my lady's maid, Letitia, join the household to continue on with me."

"Oh of course not," he responded, "Have you had the chance to acquaint yourself with the house?" He enquired to the girl.

Quickly bobbing into a curtsey, the maid spoke, "Yes, your lordship. I have been given the tour and the maids kindly allowed me to advise on how her ladyship would like her particulars arranged."

"Jolly good, I shall therefore leave my wife in your safe hands as I am sure she would like to rest and acquaint herself with her rooms."

My wife. How odd that sounded coming from his mouth.

Xander promptly removed Connie's hand from his arm as he dismissed the staff and excused himself, no doubt the lady and her maid remained stood in surprise at his rudeness. On a normal day he would attempt to be hospitable for the sake of propriety but not today. Today he needed nothing more than a stiff drink.

Striding into his study, Xander was startled to see Robert Calvert sat, feet resting on his desk and holding a glass of what appeared to be his finest brandy. Wearing the smuggest of grins, Calvert spoke mockingly, "Hello duckie."

"There is a spot," said Xander, "located in the deepest, darkest and most depraved recess of hell that has your name on it, placed there by Lucifer himself."

Calvert was clearly amused, "Most depraved, eh? Sounds rather enjoyable if I do say so myself."

"You will take your place there if you do not explain to me now why you are sat in my office, drinking my best brandy without leave on my wedding day."

"And why are you in your office, no doubt aspiring to drink your best brandy, on your wedding day?"

"I asked you first!" Shutting the door behind him, Xander strode to pour a glass for himself. Before he took a seat on the other side of the desk, he made sure to shove Calvert's feet off said piece of furniture and made a mental note to have the staff burn it.

"Was it a touching ceremony? I imagine there was a great deal of tears?"

"You would know if you were there. Which is another question for you to answer: Why were you not in attendance?"

A low chuckle emitted from his friend's throat, "Did you know this is the first society wedding I have been invited to? I decided that rather than witness a load of boring old vows even us commonfolk have the privilege of saying, I would rather be witness to the bedding ceremony instead."

Calvert paused to take a sip before pointing his finger at Xander as he continued, "Now that is without a doubt one of the finest ideas you aristocrats have had. You come for a holy ceremony and end up watching a sordid show, very delightful indeed."

Xander removed his jacket and rolled up his sleeves as he allowed his friend to prattle on. Silently he began to plot how he would exact his revenge at Calvert's nuptials.

"Of course, it is all covered up with the pretence of ensuring that the marriage is consummated. You do not have to worry about that though, or do you? Can one consummate a marriage prior to the event, or does that not count?"

The question was ignored. "Are you going to tell me why you are here, or should I call to have you forcibly removed?"

"Liam and I have a bet of how long it would take you before you came in search of drink. Unfortunately, I have lost."

"Can you please just give me an honest answer for once?"

"That is the bloody answer," Calvert exclaimed, "I wish it were not for the sake of my finances, but it is."

"And naturally you must miss the wedding to keep time I see." He paused to take a sip, "I do hope it was a hefty sum."

Calvert's grin spread even wider, "Scandalously hefty."

"Good."

Xander shut his eyes as he ran his hand through his hair in frustration. Although he would not admit it, he was thankful his friend was here to distract him from the woman currently located somewhere in the house.

"That awful, was it?" Calvert's deep voice broke through his musings. Opening his eyes and looking up to the ceiling, Xander sighed.

"I spent the ceremony fantasizing about pushing her onto one of the benches. Then, in the carriage, I seriously considered pushing her to her knees and teaching her lesson on what her mouth can do."

He closed his eyes again, "All I can think about is fucking her until she cannot remember her own name.........and I forget mine."

"*Fucking?*" Calvert queried, "That's a new one."

"The only word I can think of that reflects precisely how crude and debauched my thoughts towards her are."

Calvert took a moment to consider his words. "You could have her you know." Xander met his eyes, "Legally it's your right and, well, from all I know of the girl, she wouldn't stop you."

Xander wordlessly shook his head in refusal. "For Christ's sake man before you found out you were not the intended recipient of that note you would not stop prattling on about how receptive the girl was."

"She was receptive to another man not to me." Xander rested his elbows on his knees as he took his face in his hands. "We can keep going round in circles about that night, but the fact of the matter is Connie has been forced into a marriage with a man she does not know, nor does she want. I refuse to add to that by forcing myself on her!"

Calvert regarded his friend, "Can I give you your first piece of marriage advice my friend?"

Exasperated, Xander looked up.

"Never speak for how your wife feels unless you actually know it." Calvert spoke slowly, "Women are mystifying creatures and until you actually ask you won't know how she feels."

"And when did you become an expert on marriage?"

"When you're hopelessly in love with a woman who keeps her feelings to herself, you learn that asking is a far better method than assuming."

A swell of sympathy rushed over Xander at his friend's words. "Everything except the one question you desperately wish to ask. Am I correct?!

Calvert smiled sadly, "Speak to your wife. I'll wager she feels just as guilty about trapping you into marriage."

Leaning back in his chair, Xander considered his friends words. This wedding night would perhaps be more hopeful than he thought.

Connie resolved that the next time she spoke to her mother, she would thank her profusely for suggesting that Letitia join the Sutton household and remain with her. Lord knows how she would have felt if she had been completely surrounded by strangers in her new home.

She had initially been surprised that her new husband had so eagerly deserted her upon arrival at the house but after thinking on it, concluded that he liked nothing more than to avoid any awkward conversations.

After all, upon their first official introduction, he informed her that they would marry and then promptly left. Clearly this was not to be the loving marriage she had always dreamt of.

Letitia had guided her to her new rooms where she sat Connie down to unpin her hair and loosen her gown so she may rest. The rest did not come, however, until at least half an hour later as she had immediately burst into tears and divulged all her worries to the maid.

Marrying a stranger would not be so bad if he gave any hint of comfort to her in their brief encounters. She would have given anything to have his fingers softly brush hers as he slipped the ring on her finger or a playful tap of his knee to hers in the carriage. But no, instead her looked at her with the most intense gaze that Connie felt as though he were willing her to drop dead on the spot.

She could not blame him. If it were not for her foolish actions at the ball, he would not have married her in the first place. He would have been happily living his bachelor life instead of being stuck married to a girl who trapped him into marriage. No doubt fulfilling the impressions he and the Ainsworth clan would have about her.

After she rested, Connie took a light supper in her room, fearing what she would come across if she dared leave her sanctuary. She then called on Letitia to query all the details of the house she would need as the new mistress.

Unfortunately for Connie, it appeared that there would be little she could do that would not put her in direct cross hairs with her new mother-in-law, the dowager countess. She was informed that the woman preferred the house to be run exactly to her liking and if she saw anything that she had not personally approved of the housekeeper, Mrs Potter, would be immediately called into the drawing room where shrieks would be heard from. This was always followed by a dismissal of one of the staff.

Connie had to consider the softest approach to resolve this. She had heard stories before of mistresses so terrible that they were eventually unable to obtain decent servants and so were reduced to hiring complete novices practically off the street to work in the household.

Yes, this would need to be dealt with quickly.

Before Connie realised how late it was, the clock struck ten and she was assisted out of her wedding dress and into a nightgown of sheer silk from her reticule. Despite the lack of time to prepare, the Duchess of Bristol had somehow procured a full wardrobe of new clothes for her daughter to begin married life with.

Thinking of the dresses made her smile, as Connie knew she would now be able to wear colours not previously permitted to her. Unmarried ladies would often be required to wear pale colours such as blues and whites. Now, a whole world of colours was opened to her.

Settling into bed, Connie was struck by the realisation that her husband would join her in bed. He appeared so indifferent to her since his arrival at Wexford House that she did not believe he would wish to come to her bed.

Now that the night had arrived, however, she could not help but feel a sense of delightful apprehension. It was true that the majority of her thoughts the past month were filled with worry regarding her circumstances but when she was alone in her bed, trying to sleep, the memories of their tryst would return to her. On one occasion the lust she felt at the memory left her writhing with need and not knowing how to resolve it.

Connie found herself wishing that her husband would join her soon. The anticipation left her body tingling.

She turned as she heard the door adjoining their bedrooms open and he appeared, dressed in a green dressing gown over a loose, white shirt. Connie could not help but stare at the exposed triangle of his chest. Dark hairs were scattered across him, she felt the urge to reach out and run her hands across him, feeling the brush of the hairs over his firm chest. She bit her lip to stop the moan that threatened to erupt at the sight of him.

Lifting her head, she met Xander's eyes and recognised the same dark intensity she saw that night in the gallery. She suddenly needed to take deeper breaths as she felt her legs unconsciously part in need of him.

Their shared gaze felt like it lasted a lifetime, the raw lust rising between them. Feeling the same desperate need she felt that night, Connie had one thought echoing through her mind.

Claim me.

Just as Connie opening her mouth to voice that one thought, his filled the air.

"My apologies for the intrusion, we do not wish to bring any more gossip to our doorstep than we already have" he looked away from her "and if I do not sleep in your bed tonight the servants will surely talk."

Trying to project an air of nonchalance, Connie smiled at her husband. "Of course, my lord, it is your husbandly right after all."

His back had turned to her as he went to remove his robe and he stilled in his actions as he registered her meaning. Slowly, he continued to undress. Now remaining only in his nightshirt, he turned back to her.

"As long as the servants believe what we wish them to believe, it is of no consequence that sleeping will be the only action to occur in this bed tonight."

He might as well have doused her with a bucket of cold water, Connie thought. Clearly her earlier perceptions were correct as he had no desire for her whatsoever.

Connie lay back against the pillows and then turned onto her side, facing away from him. She felt the bed dip behind her, and a jolt of coldness met her backside as he raised the bedsheets. This was soon replaced by the heat from his body.

Connie definitely would not be sleeping well tonight.

The bed shifted as he blew out the candles on his side and the pair lay in stilted silence. Clearly aware of each other's presence and not knowing how to proceed.

Unable to bear the silence any longer, Connie had to say something but, not knowing the man well enough, she struggled to find exactly what she should say.

"Goodnight my lord, sleep well." Connie mentally kicked herself at her inability to even attempt to speak to her husband in anything other than platitudes.

"Goodnight Constance." Came the low murmur of his response. It sent shivers down her spine as she imagined him saying her name in an altogether different fashion in this bed.

Resolving to ignore the temptation behind her, Connie closed her eyes and willed sleep to take over.

Chapter Ten

The morning after the wedding Xander opted to slip out of bed before Connie woke. It was not a chore to rise before her as Xander had spent the entire night chasing a sleep that would not come.

As he poured his morning coffee in the dining room, Xander reflected on his complete failure to make any sort of progress the night before. He had intended to follow Calvert's advice and have an honest discussion with his wife in the hopes that it would lead to a warm rapport and a good marriage. His plans flew out the window the second he walked through the bedroom door and observed Connie sat up in bed, locks cascading over her shoulders and wearing a negligee that left little to the imagination.

All coherent thought left his mind, and it took all his willpower to stop himself from launching at the unsuspecting woman and ravishing her there and then. Xander instead decided that he would wait until morning and begin the conversation when his wife was more appropriately attired. He was trying to show her that he was not a monster who took advantage of innocent maidens after all, and what he wanted to do the night before would not help him in that area.

Connie entered the room when he was partway through his breakfast, greeting him with a cautious smile.

"Good morning husband, I hope you slept well." Typically, Xander was in the middle of chewing a sausage and so could only respond in over-exaggerated nods for several seconds as he pointed to his mouth.

His wife appeared to be stifling a laugh as she poured herself tea and proceeded to select food for her breakfast.

"Is your mother not joining us for breakfast this morning? I was under the impression she resided here as well."

Xander cleared his throat before responding, "No, she usually takes her breakfast in bed. I admit I believed you would as well, is it not usually the case for married ladies to do so?"

Connie's face dropped and she appeared disappointed at his words. Hope suddenly welled up in Xander's chest.

"Oh, did you not wish for me to join you? I can always arrange for the future to…"

"Please stay," he hastily interrupted, "I often find it quite lonely in the mornings. Your company is much appreciated."

She gazed at him as she tentatively took her seat. "I am glad to hear that. I fear I would feel rather sluggish if I ate in bed. I would also enjoy being in your company too." The last sentenced was spoken so softly Xander feared he misheard her. He chose to believe he heard right and beamed in response.

"I must be honest that is a great relief to hear." Xander decided to slowly begin his approach, "I had feared that you thought me frightful."

Connie's eyebrows furrowed in confusion at his words. "Why ever would you think that?" she enquired.

His eyes quickly darted to the two footmen present as he considered how to speak candidly. "Perhaps we could spend the day together?" He changed the subject, considering how they could find some privacy. "A walk in Regent's Park might be nice?" *And full of nosy well-wishers too!*

The unamused look on her face was discerning. "It's raining too much for a walk and you are changing the subject."

"I only meant that we could do some activity that would afford us privacy to speak freely."

"We are in the privacy of your home, why can we not speak freely now?"

"We could easily be overheard.........and it is our home now."

Xander almost missed her response as she pursed her lips, drawing his eyes to them and making the desire to kiss them return.

"But you are the lord and master and if you wish for privacy, you can tell the servants to leave the room at once." Her eyes glinted and eyebrows lifted in a challenge.

"Rule number one about having servants, my dear wife, is that you will never have privacy. Loyalty yes but privacy never. And as long as my blasted mother is about the former will never come about either, I am afraid."

Connie appeared to consider her thoughts. Xander hoped he had convinced her to take a different approach.

"We could always go to bed!" Xander chocked on his coffee in surprise. That was not the approach he had imagined she would take.

He practically spluttered his words out "I hardly think going to bed should solve our problems." Images raced across his mind of Connie naked underneath him......and on top of him.

"Well, no one would dare disturb us there. We could speak quite freely." Xander ran his hand through his hair in frustration and his wife casually sipped her tea and took smile bites of toast.

"Clearly you have never heard of voyeurism" he muttered under his breath.

"What was that dear?"

"Nothing," Xander gave himself ten seconds to close his eyes and fight for some semblance of sanity before he resumed the conversation. "I know you may think otherwise and indeed you may be correct. But it is my belief that there is no part of the home whatsoever we could go to without the eyes and ears of the servants being upon us. Hence why I would prefer it if we found some activity outside of the house where we could speak freely to one another."

Connie bit her lip as she gathered her response. It appeared to Xander that she was having some sort of conflict of her own on how to speak with him.

Connie's eyes appeared beseeching as they met his once again. "I honestly would quite like to…"

Jennings suddenly appeared holding a silver tray with a note resting on it.

"My apologies for the interruption my lord but a message has arrived from Lord William Ainsworth."

Irritated at the interruption Xander snapped at his butler. "Whatever it is it can wait!"

"I am afraid sir that there appears to have been a fire at the printing press and your guidance has been urgently requested."

Blast! Xander thought, it must be serious if Liam was requesting his presence there. Something small and Calvert would be able to handle it on his own but anything that required all three men was unavoidable.

He took the note and skimmed through it before turning back to his wife.

"My apologies, Constance, I really would stay but they would not disturb me unless it was important."

"Just go" came the curt reply. Xander blinked in surprise before hastily rising. Out of the corner of his eye he could see Jennings had now gone to the front door to retrieve his coat and hat from a footman.

He began to walk to the door before pausing and then changing direction until he stood before his wife. Having no clue how to fix the upset he had clearly caused her, Xander bent and gave a swift kiss to Connie's cheek.

"We will talk later, I promise." As he left the room Xander resolved to arrange for several hundred flowers to be sent to his wife before he returned.

I honestly would quite like to go to bed with you in any case.........and not talk!

That had been what Connie had intended to say to her departing husband before they were interrupted.

She had woken that morning to find his place in the bed already empty and cold. The disappointed feeling that ran through her was one that she had no desire to feel again and so Connie resolved to take matters into her own hands.

Recalling some conversation she had once overheard between her brothers about the easy rapport that comes immediately after bedding a woman, Connie decided the best course of action would be to somehow entice her husband to bed as soon as possible.

When she saw him initially upon entering the dining room, Connie almost waivered but somehow, she twisted the conversation to the bedroom. There was a brief flash in his eyes where she could tell he was imagining them in bed together, but he tried to pull the subject away.

Not to be swayed, Connie opted to come right out and say that she wanted him in her bed making love to her, not caring that the servants heard her.

Of course, in typical Constance fashion, she would not be able to finish her request and now she was sat alone and entirely unsure of how to continue. Blanching at how she failed in her attempt at seduction, if you could even call it that, Connie promptly whined and rested her head on the table with a resounding thud.

Even worse was that, when Connie finally lifted her head, her eyes immediately met a footman who was clearly in shock over her thoroughly unladylike display.

Taking a breath to gather what was left of her dignity, Connie then proceeded to finish her breakfast as she mulled over the best steps to take.

Connie lamented that her closest friends were all unmarried maidens who would not be able to offer any advice on the art of seduction. Her cousins both resided primarily in the country which ruled them out as help. Her thoughts briefly turned to her mother, which made Connie cringe. Cora Wexford had done a good and thorough job of explaining what is to be expected of a married woman, but Connie did not dare consider approaching her for this task. She imagined it would lead to several horrifying moments when she would not be able to help but imagine her mother using those same suggestions on her father.

Connie shuddered at the thought.

A thought then came to Connie that gave her pause. She had three brothers after all and from the gossip she heard she knew they were popular with women. Why not ask one of them for advice.

Naturally, the brother she would speak to was Duncan, Connie considered. Matt is clearly lacking when it comes to marital relations whilst Harry, at the tender age of nineteen, may be too young to be taken seriously. Not to mention he was due to leave for his post in a few days.

Duncan had always been the brother she had gone to in times of trouble. Connie knew she could trust him to take her question seriously and to keep it private. Grinning, Connie rose and went in search of Letitia to assist in preparing her to go out.

The look on Lord Duncan Wexford's face was most certainly not optimistic. Somehow, Connie lamented, he managed to not only appear as if his nose had picked up some offending odour, but he had also gone pale, eyes widened in terror and seemed as if he may empty the contents of his stomach at any moment.

Shifting uncomfortably in her seat, Connie lost her patience. "Well, are you going to help me or not?" She snapped.

Slowly leaning forward, her brother began, "Just so I am positively clear in all of this. You, my little sister, have decided to come to my bachelor lodgings unaccompanied this morning, risking scandal might I add with that, force me out of my bed, where a lady friend I have no desire for you to meet currently rests, and have asked me to provide to you, from my alcohol-induced haze-ridden mind, a suggestion of methods for you to employ to lure your husband to your bed?"

"Yes, I feel that is an accurate summation of events." Connie responded.

Gaping in shock horror, Duncan rose as went to a table holding several beverages. Connie could just make out his mutterings as referencing her being the death of him through driving him to drink.

Duncan downed a glass of port then proceeded to pour himself another. Returning to his seat, he thrust his index finger to her. "Why in god's name would you think I want anything to do with your bedroom activities?"

Connie rolled her eyes. "I do not think, nor do I want you to have anything to do with them. I am simply asking you for some advice on how to attract my husband."

"You did a good enough job the first time. Why should you need any help now?"

"Because, brother, I do not have a mask to hide behind this time. And besides, I thought I was inviting a man I knew to a tryst which makes a difference."

Duncan scratched his chin in consideration. "You are in a situation of your own doing young lady and you can get yourself out of it." A grin suddenly appeared on his face, "Maybe you should ask the Ainsworth's for their opinion, you are stuck with them now."

Connie saw she would need to provoke her brother into helping her. "You know, I think you may be onto something there. The Duke of Bristol does have a reputation with the women after all. He should be a great deal of help to me."

Promptly rising, Connie strode across the room until a hand gripping her arm stopped her. Looking up at her brother's face, Connie met his challenging stare.

After several moments of unspoken tension, Duncan rolled his eyes and released his sister as he slumped into his chair in resignation.

With a victorious smile, Connie gracefully returned to the chaise she had vacated and flattened her skirts.

"Now dear brother, are you going to offer some tea?"

"No." Came the grumpy reply.

Exasperated at her brother's person, Connie went straight to the point. "Well, you may as well realise that the sooner you decide to help me, the sooner I will leave, and you can go back to Miss………."

"She's actually a Mrs if you must know." Duncan crossed his arms, "You want my honest advice?"

"Please Duncan," Connie beseeched, "I know you do not approve but I need to reach the man somehow."

Duncan sighed, "All I want is for you to be happy, sister. I suppose for that to occur I must traumatise myself." The pair exchanged warm smiles before he continued.

"It is quite simple really, just be obvious about what you want, and he'll come running."

Connie blinked in confusion, "Obvious? How should I be obvious?"

"It is as I said: quite simple. Men are not overly complicated figures, regardless of what you may believe, we prefer to get straight to the point. When you see him, do not dawdle just go sit on his lap or run your hands along his chest and say 'darling, take me to bed.' If that does not work undress in front of him, that should make it clear enough what you want."

Connie's mouth dropped. "That all sounds rather uncouth."

"Yes, you are absolutely correct." Duncan stretched his legs, "But I can tell you something little one, if I had a wife and she told me straight that she wanted me in her bed that moment, wild horses could not keep me from it."

"You know you are not doing your kind any favours with this?" Connie answered, "It seems to be that you are under the impression that all men are so easily manipulated."

Her brother's laugh echoed around the room, "It's not that we're easily manipulated just that coy glances and subtle hints go over our heads."

Connie rose from her seat, "Well, thank you for this enlightening information. I shall be sure to keep it in mind."

Seeing her to the door, Duncan paused before he opened it, "Just do me one favour, Connie dear."

"And what is that?"

"Don't tell me how it goes."

Chapter Eleven

Upon her return to the house, Connie was disappointed to learn that her husband had not yet returned. Worry crossed her features as she considered how serious the fire must have been to keep Xander away when he seemed so determined to spend time with her, bickering and all.

Instead, she chose to use her free time by exploring her new home. The housekeeper, Mrs Potter, gave her a tour of all the rooms. Connie was particularly delighted by how beautiful the gardens appeared, with a stunning display of syringas, hollyhocks and laburnums in a variety of yellows, pinks, and blues.

It was noted by Connie, however, that the opulence so magnificently displayed in the gardens appeared to be rather gaudy when inside the house. The rooms appeared to rival one another in how loud and mismatched the colours could be. Not only that, but there was not a single surface in the entire house that did not hold some sort of decoration.

Whilst all the individual pieces on their own were beautiful, the multitude of them in each room came across as cluttered and by the end of the tour Connie felt quite overstimulated.

Following a light lunch Connie was informed that her new mother-in-law had returned to the house and had requested that she be joined in the drawing room for tea. Connie cautiously entered the room, which appeared to have a colour scheme containing all the citrus fruits and greeted the Dowager Countess.

"Please, do take a seat Constance dear. After all, this is your home now too." Although her words were kind, something about Helena Chalmers' tone unnerved Connie.

Observing the woman, she could see where Xander inherited his good looks. Just like her son, the Dowager Countess' dark blue eyes bore an intensity one could not help being drawn to. Their almond shape balanced the delicately straight nose and the softness of her cheeks and mouth made the woman appear warm and inviting. But there was something about her that gave Connie the distinct impression that she should not allow herself to be reeled in.

"I must give my apologies for not showing you the house myself," the Dowager Countess began, "But I had a prior engagement at Lady Cuthbert's which I could not cancel. As a matter of fact, I have received a great deal more invitations than usual thanks to your *unexpected* nuptials." The gaze as she sipped her tea was discerning.

Connie opted not to rise to the bait. "Do not fret, Mrs Potter did a wonderful job. I must say the gardens were rather enchanting."

"Yes well, the gardens were designed by my late husband's grandmother. They became rather notable, and guests still ask to see them. They are not to my taste but, alas, who am I to anger the public?"

She appeared so sincere in her belief that they were famous among the Ton, although Connie had never heard on them. Connie masked her surprise by taking a large gulp of tea. As long as the gardens were kept as they were, she did not mind her mother-in-law's delusions continuing.

"Well, I firmly understand the impressions it gives among the general populace." Connie swallowed her nerves for her next statement. "I did make a few mental notes on some small changes I would like to make if you would be kind enough to guide me on the best methods of redecoration."

The laugh in response was shrill, "Oh little girl, no you shan't be making any changes. I led the redecorating and have created a house of great notability".

It took all the strength in Connie not to roll her eyes. She attempted to softly sway her mother-in-law, "But do you not think that the house is not in keeping with the fashion of today? I believe it is more in style to be…" she gazed around the room "subtle."

"My dear, fashion is for today, grandeur is forever!" Never before had Connie heard such ridiculous words of delusion.

"With all due respect *Dowager* Countess, I am the lady of the house now and I shall make any changes I see fit." Connie had to summon all her courage when confronted with the daggers coming from the woman sat opposite her.

"Just because you have the title of the current Countess of Sutton does not mean that you hold any power." The response came through lips pursed in amusement, "In this household I have the experience and the natural aura of the head of the house."

"Just because you have never had another woman to challenge your authority does not mean you have the ability to keep it."

"My apologies, did you just call yourself a woman? You are nothing but a naïve little chit who has no experience and no right to say she can run a household."

"I merely said that I wished to make some minor changes to the design of the house with the request of your guidance out of respect and immediately your response has been to name-call and mock. I hardly think you are any authority on whether a person has the character to lead."

"Oh, you think what I have said is mocking? Well, little girl, let me truly tell you what it is I think," came the mocking reply. "First of all, a seventeen-year-old child has no place running a household. Secondly, my son is the current holder of a title almost five hundred years old. You come from a family of upstarts who have no true sense of what it is like to be associated with that sort of grandeur. After all, your mother was practically the daughter of a farmer."

Connie could not even compose her defence of her family in her head before the woman moved on.

"Not only is your family full of upstarts and social climbers but it is the holder of circumstances that have bred you and your brothers for failure! No one marries for love child; they may find a sense of agreeableness with their spouse but anyone of actual notability does not allow themselves to be tainted by love. Look at what it has done for your brother already, the boy has been made a cuckold several times over because he has no clue on how to conduct himself in a proper marriage."

Connie refused to believe the lies spewing from the woman's mouth. Matt and Jane may not be happy in their marriage, but Jane would not do that to her husband.

"And then you most certainly have not fallen into a lovestruck marriage yourself, have you? I know my son. Like many others his age he is a boy who has shown no desire to marry. He has enjoyed sowing his wild oats far too much. Not that marriage is going to stop him taking any lovers." Connie began to feel sick. "So, one must consider why a man with no intentions of marriage would suddenly obtain a special license and marry in haste. Well," she pointed her finger to

Constance, "I think it quite obvious that you trapped my son into marriage. His behaviour today should be enough evidence. Rather than going on a honeymoon with his young, new bride, he has decided to go to his club with his friends."

Connie could not have felt more pained had it been a physical slap rather than a verbal one. The sad thing was Connie knew all the last part to be true. She had trapped an innocent man into marriage, and she would be trapped in the knowledge for the rest of her life.

Whilst she was sympathetic to her husband, however, it did not extend to the witch sat opposite her. And so, Connie resolved to remind the woman how her position had changed.

Trying to appear nonchalant, Connie responded, "I shall refrain from responding to your words as they are both too false and too ridiculous for me to consider."

She opted not to pause for effect once she saw the woman's mouth move to respond. "Besides, the fact remains that I am the Countess of Sutton and official lady of the household now and should you wish to retain your position of privilege you had best give up your fight for control."

"Never!" The response did not surprise Connie.

"Then we have nothing more to discuss." Connie rose in preparation of leaving. "For all we know, I could be carrying my husband's heir as we speak and if you wish to have any relation to your future grandchildren you shall cease your coldness and begin co-operating. Good day madam."

As Connie walked towards the door, she was sure she had won the disagreement, but the Dowager Countess' final words caused her to stumble.

"I am sure when that baby arrives a month early and in perfect health you shall be very gratified by my silence. After you have earned it though."

She maintained a cool façade as she ventured through the house to her rooms where upon closing the bedroom door behind her, Connie collapsed onto the bed and took deep breaths to slow her shaking.

Once her composure had been regained, at least somewhat, Connie mentally composed her next plan of action. Clearly, she would need to make as many allies as possible if her mother-in-law proved to be as much of an opponent as she had promised to be.

From the gossip passed by Letitia, Connie knew all she would need to do is be kind and fair to have the servants on her side. Jennings and Mrs Potter would need to be spoken to ensuring that any formal decisions for the house be directly brought to her.

The main challenge would be the technical head of the household though. Xander may prove his mother correct and allow any resentment felt towards Connie to fester. After all, it was true that he had been trapped into marriage.

Connie became more determined than ever to win her husband over. When she woke this morning, she simply wanted a husband. Now it seemed, she would need him to be an ally.

Xander was contemplating the best method to dispose of a body.

Upon his arrival at the factory used for his printing press investments, he was confused to find that there was no emergency at all. This was followed by terror causing adrenaline to rush around his body as a hood was placed over his head and he felt several pairs of arms grab at him and shove him into what he perceived to be a carriage that quickly began to move.

Recovering from the shock, he began to demand answers from his kidnappers. His shouts were met with silence. He then began to plot his next move. Unfortunately, his hands were tied behind his back, preventing him from removing the hood.

He considered somehow struggling free and running from the carriage once it had stopped, his legs and feet were not bound, but that plan was soon scrapped when he realised that the most likely conclusion to that escape attempt would be him running headfirst into a lamppost. After all, Xander was the type of person that would happen to.

Xander rued that he would have to wait until he at least had his vision returned to take any action. He kept his ears open for any clue as to who his kidnappers were.

After what seemed to be at least thirty minutes, the carriage jolted to a sudden halt and Xander was once again lifted and carried out. When he was being brought through what seemed to be a hallway the event began to make sense. One of the men carrying his legs almost dropped him to the ground and promptly burst out.

"Gods, you did not tell me he was this heavy!"

Lord Frederick Ainsworth.

A moment of relief came over him as he realised his abductors had no malicious intent. This quickly turned to anger as he considered that his friends had tricked him into leaving his new bride for their own amusement. He therefore began to devise the various methods he would use to kill his so-called friends, hence why he now was trying to concoct how to dispose of the bodies.

Xander was suddenly thrust onto a sofa and could hear some shuffling around him. He blinked as the hood was swept from his head and he could finally take in his surroundings.

He recognised the private room as being in their favourite club to haunt, Boodles, and his anger was briefly turned into bemusement as he saw the way Liam, Calvert and

Freddie appeared to be jigging in their presentation of the room.

Xander closed his eyes, took a deep breath, and counted to ten. An act he repeated upon seeing his friends still jigging when his eyes opened. The second attempt to quell his anger seemed to work.

"I advise that you tell me why you abducted me the morning after my wedding before you untie me as I plan to pummel all of you!"

Liam answered whilst waving his arms around the room, "Welcome, my dear friend, to your bachelor party." The point was complimented the *pop* of a champagne bottle being opened by Calvert with a "*Huzza!*"

"Does not one have to be a bachelor for that?" Xander dryly responded.

"I shall answer your question with one of my own," Calvert moved to bring the bottle and glasses over, "did you heed my advice and resolve your marriage woes last night."

Xander swallowed as he realised, he needed that drink more than ever. "Untie me and give me a drink and I shall tell you."

With a nod of his brother's head, Freddie got up and drew a knife to cut the rope on his hands. As soon as Xander felt his hands free, he swung his elbow up, not caring what he hit.

Freddie staggered back to his seat and delved into his pocket to retrieve a handkerchief to hold to his nose.

"Look at this," he said, moving the fabric from his nose to his line of sight, "I'm bleeding!"

Liam gave him a firm pat on the shoulder as he handed his brother a glass. "And that, baby brother, is why Calvert and I were so insistent that you be the one to release Sutton."

"Schoolboy error," Calvert handed Xander a glass before taking his own seat, "Come on then chap, why are your balls still blue then?"

Xander downed his glass before answering, "I fully intended to do as you said and confront Constance as to our troubles. I walked in that bedroom preparing to reassure her that I was not a monster and she had nothing to fear from me. And then………"

He looked up to see three pairs of eyes looking expectantly at him. Xander stood to pour himself another glass and opted to take the bottle back with him as he returned to his seat. He raised the glass to his lips as he finished the sentence. "She was wearing a nightgown so sheer I could see her nipples and the monster came back." The second glass was downed.

Liam looked perplexed, "So, did you, or didn't you?"

"My balls are bloody bluer than virgin-boy over there." Xander loosely waved his arm towards Freddie as he slouched into his chair in defeat.

"I am not a virgin I will have you know!" Liam clearly did not believe his brother as he placated him, "Of course you're not Freddie, we obviously believe you. Now Sutton, why are you being such a fool and not seducing your wife?"

Xander glared at his friend. "Believe it or not, it's not actually that simple a thing to do."

"Otherwise, Matthew Wexford would have a much more pleasant demeanour." Calvert smirked.

Not to be discouraged, Liam continued, "Listen, old friend, I am the last person to offer compliments. But you actually are rather good where women are concerned."

Xander did not fail to notice how the other two men in the room were sniggering.

"Now, all of us in this room are perfectly aware that you are a bumbling idiot," "Many thanks." "You're welcome but as I was saying, you are rather good at tricking people into thinking that you are all dark and brooding when you do that thing."

Liam then began gesturing two of his fingers back and forth from his face to Xander's. Xander was utterly bemused at his friend and began to imitate him. "What is this? What are you doing? Is this some kind of hand twitch you have developed?" He furrowed his brows in confusion.

Liam suddenly snapped his fingers and pointed as he exclaimed "That's it! That's that thing you do that makes the ladies go *ooooh*."

Calvert guffawed, "Please repeat that noise, you sounded most convincing."

"Shut up!" Liam snapped "See to us you look as if you have lost brain cells, but women genuinely think you're handsome when you do that."

With his eyes darting back and forth between the three men nodding in agreement, Xander mused aloud, "I was popular in school, how have I ended up with this crowd as my closest friends?"

"I can answer that," Calvert interrupted his thoughts, "You like me as I make you rich and Liam's insulting humour makes you laugh. Oh, and Liam's mother said he has to bring Freddie along because he struggles to make friends and is a virgin."

"For the last time I am not a virgin!" Freddie was ignored by the other men as they continued to debate Xander's ability to seduce his wife.

Deciding he wanted the conversation to stop, Xander shouted over the others, "FINE! I shall return home and promptly inform my wife I have no plans to force her to bed and will not touch her without her giving me leave to do so. I will additionally find some way of not being a bumbling imbecile around her and actually get to know the woman so we can at least attempt to be happy together."

"Let's drink to that!" Freddie's toast was followed by a chorus of *hear hears* and *jolly goods*.

Later on, whilst Xander was in the process of opening the fourth bottle, Calvert leaned towards Liam and said under his breath, "Are you sure this plan will work?"

Liam's mouth moved to a smug smile as he responded, "Positive. After all, I'd be more shocked if Sutton did not do his usual spilling out his feelings to anyone who will listen tonight."

"One more bottle should do it," Calvert watched his friend over his glass, "then we can deliver him to his wife."

"Just to be safe we'll start the conversation. I must say though, seeing the horror on that pretty little face will be rather amusing." Liam rubbed his hands in glee.

Chapter Twelve

Connie was spending her afternoon reading when she heard a commotion coming from the entrance of the house. Cautiously making her way to the source of the noise, she stopped in her tracks upon being greeted by the sight of her husband being held up by two of his friends as he attempted to walk.

Gaping at the scene before her, Connie began to silently walk backwards in the hopes of escaping the men. Her plans were unfortunately thwarted when her inebriated husband spotted her.

"CONNIE!" Xander made a staggered jog towards his wife and promptly enveloped her in an overpowering embrace before turning back to his friends, pulling his wife with him. "Gentlemen, have you met my beautiful wife?" His speech slurred.

"My apologies Countess," Liam Ainsworth nodded to her, "our plan did not involve this much drink."

Before Liam could say any more, Xander pressed a finger to his friend's lips with a "*Ssshh.*"

A fair-haired gentleman Connie did not recognise rubbed his hand over his eyes as he spoke, "Yes, your wife obviously believes that you are sober in this moment."

Xander dopily grinned and nodded, clearly believing he was fooling her. Connie began to roll her eyes, but her husband lost his balance leaning into her and she had to regain her footing to prevent the two of them falling to the ground.

Not seeming to worry about being unable to stand straight, Xander said "Do you know what he said about me? Callert said I was a bumbling idiot!"

"No, I believe I, *Calvert,* said you were a buffoon. Liam said you were an idiot." The man Connie could now identify as Calvert said.

"Who said it does not matter," Xander waved his arm for emphasis, "they called me a bumbling idiot. Can you believe they would call me that?" Xander gestured to his wife.

"Yes." Connie could only manage the one word, so surprised by the scene that she was. His booming laugh in response made her jump.

"She's so funny. Did you gents know my wife is funny? I have a funny wife."

"How was I funny?" Came Connie's perplexed response.

"I think we should take our leave." Liam nodded to Calvert before leaning towards Connie. "Have him lie on his front when he goes to bed with his head on its side. If you want to be nice to him in the morning, give him a hearty breakfast. But if you want to punish him, make many loud noises." His words were punctuated with a wink.

Xander playfully shoved his friend away and pointed to the door. "No! My wife! Find one of your own. Wrong Wexford!"

Connie watched the men retreat and bit her lip as she contemplated the next step to take. Although she had revelled in teasing as they recovered the following mornings, Connie had never witnessed her brothers in their cups before and had no idea what to do with the man next to her now.

Lifting her head towards her husband, Connie was startled by the dark look in his eyes that appeared to be directed to her mouth.

Hastily releasing her lip, Connie cleared her throat which appeared to bring Xander out of his haze.

"Perhaps we should get you to bed?" Xander rapidly blinked at her before a wide grin spread over his face.

"That is the best idea I have heard all day." Connie had no intentions of enacting what she could tell was running through her husband's mind but deduced that the best way to get him to sleep off the drink would be to make him think that was what she wanted.

It took approximately twenty minutes to have Xander successfully climb the stairs and a further five to reach the bedroom. Connie believed the most difficult task would be to stop her husband pawing his hands at her once the bedroom was reached. Luckily, he immediately collapsed headfirst onto the bed and began snoring.

After removing his shoes and laying a blanket on his sleeping form, Connie took a moment to watch over her husband.

She gently ran her hand through his hair and softly smiled as he sighed at the contact. Connie stifled a laugh as she realised that she had managed to do the task she set out for herself for the day. She had gotten her husband into her bed, just not in the way she wished to.

The following morning, Xander woke to find two housemaids staring at him. He blinked as his eyes adjusted to the light and sat up as he took in his surroundings.

He was horrified to realise that he had no memory of anything that followed the third bottle of champagne being opened the day before. He surmised it must have been the day before as the light shining through the bedroom window only came through so vividly in the morning.

How had he ended up in his wife's bedroom?

"Pardon me Sir," Xander's attention was brought to the taller of the two maids, "Her Ladyship bid us to wake you and request you join her for breakfast as we change the beds."

The thought of eating anything made his stomach turn. With a nod, he slowly made his way out of bed. He momentarily struggled to gain his footing, causing both maids to jump back in fear he would knock them over.

Xander was greeting by the sight of a bathtub upon entering his dressing room. In his hazed mind he patted himself on the back for somehow ending up with such a kind wife who was clearly thinking of his needs.

All such assumptions were removed from his mind the second he put his foot into the tub and realised the water was freezing cold. His accompanying shriek brought his valet running.

"Berry, you shall need to have the bathtub refilled, I am afraid the water has gone cold."

"My apologies Your Lordship, but I am afraid I cannot." Xander's head whipped to Berry, who appeared sheepish under his harsh gaze.

"And why the devil not?"

"Because, Sir, Her Ladyship specifically ask that the water be cold." The man appeared to cringe as he continued. "She also said I was to roughly scrub your back to ensure your smell would not taint her nose or her dining room."

Upon seeing Xander's dark look he hastily added, "Those were her words, My Lord."

Xander closed his eyes as he shrugged in defeat. "I deserve this, don't I?"

"Honestly, Sir, I am afraid so."

"Does she have any other punishments lined up for me?"

"I cannot say for certain, Sir, although......." His voice trailed off.

"Although?" Xander urged.

"I did overhear the words 'sloppy porridge' said to the cook." Xander had to stop himself from vomiting at the thought.

Resigned to his fate, Xander nodded his head and said, "Let's get this over with then."

After lowering himself down into the tab, Xander told his valet through chattered teeth, "Do me one favour, Berry, don't ever get married!

Breakfast with his wife did not improve Xander's prospects of a happy marriage. Every movement Connie made she appeared to be determined to be as loud as possible.

Xander did embrace his fortunes, however small, as he observed the full breakfast Connie laid before him, having insisted she serve him his food "as a good wife should."

Xander savoured the meal of bacon, sausage, eggs, and toasted bread as his wife began what he believed would be the inevitable lecture.

"Need I remind you that we are expected to attend a concert hosted by the March's tonight?" Xander grimaced at the thought. He had completely forgotten that this was to be their debut into society as husband and wife and all eyes would be on them tonight.

Swallowing his food, Xander replied, "How could I forget, darling, might I enquire as to ho…."

His wife clearly did not expect an answer from him as she continued. "I shall be out today as I am taking lunch with my mama before we collect my dress. Whilst I am gone you may do whatever it is that men do after they have been in their cups and ensure that you are fresh-faced and ready to at least pretend we are in a happy marriage tonight."

"I'll show you a happy marriage." Xander grumbled into his teacup causing Connie's head to sharply turn towards him.

"What was that?"

"I said I certainly would." He gave his wife a strained smile as she narrowed her eyes at him.

"Well, I must take my leave, enjoy your day."

Connie promptly stood and walked out the door without looking back at him. Xander groaned and banged his head upon the table. Somewhere in his still-addled mind he swore he heard a muttered query of something being an everyday occurrence.

Connie was sitting at her dressing table, ensuring there were no stray hairs when her husband opened the door to beckon her to the carriage.

She rose and stalked past him silently, the skirts of her violet gown swishing behind her. It appeared he would rather walk behind her as they strode down the hall.

"I gather you are still angry with me?"

Connie span on her heel to turn to Xander. Seeing him casually stood looking at her with his hands in his pockets caused all the anger and annoyance to rise and lash out at him.

"Am I still angry with you? Is that an actual question? Are you genuinely asking me that?" He opened his mouth to respond then sheepishly shut it as she continued.

"NO! Do not dare speak back to me right now!" Her chest was heaving as she unleashed all the feelings that had run through her the past few days.

"You told me you had an emergency with one of your investments. You left me to go drinking with your friends the day after our wedding. You left me not two minutes after saying you wanted to spend the day with me and build a foundation for our marriage."

Xander bowed his head in what Connie hoped was complete and utter shame.

"I honestly do not know why I should be surprised. Is this not how you have behaved every moment we have been together?"

Her eyes began to well up as she looked at him. "When you came to propose you stayed less than five minutes and then I did not see you until I was walking down the aisle. I thought you would at least try at the start."

"I had wanted you to be there calling on me during our engagement. I had wanted you to willingly come to my bed. I had wanted to spend my first day as a marrie........."

Connie was prevented from finishing as Xander suddenly pushed her against a wall a claimed her mouth in a heart-stopping kiss.

Overcoming a brief moment of surprise, Connie grasped his shoulders to pull his body against hers as she opened her mouth to tangle her tongue with his.

His hands kneaded her buttocks through her skirts, causing her to moan into his mouth. Pushing herself further into him, Connie felt his growing hardness and began to desperately grind her crotch against his, needing more of him.

After what felt like an eternity, Xander pulled his head away from her to look into her eyes, keeping her body enclosed against the wall in his.

His voice was husky as he spoke, "Did you want me to come to your bed because it was your wifely duty or because you want me?"

Connie moistened her lips as she answered, "I wanted you. I haven't been able to stop thinking about how you felt inside me."

She held her breath as she waited for his response to her honesty. The way he furrowed his brow and stared firmly at her gave her a tingling sensation that shot straight to her breasts and pelvis. Connie was sure she must be red all over from the heat emitting between the pair of them.

"You want me?"

"How could I not when you look at me like that?"

"Confused?" A breathy laugh left her lips at his response. Sensing that she would need to convince her husband further, Connie began to slowly run her gloved hands over his shoulders and down his chest.

He closed his eyes as he felt her ministrations. Choosing to be even bolder, Connie trailed her hands around his hips until they rested on his behind and gently nudged them forward to come into direct contact with her crotch.

Xander rested his head against the wall beside hers as he began to slowly rock his hips against hers.

"We should be on our way to the March's at this moment." He said between shallow breaths.

"Yes, we should." Connie sighed.

"You really should stop me."

"No, I shouldn't." His response was to groan and grind harder against her. Connie teased him further by slightly turning her head and lightly biting his neck.

Xander began to bunch up her skirts in his hands as he spoke. "Give me a reason to stop right now."

Connie did not need to answer as a voice was heard from the bottom of the stairs.

"YOU HAVE TEN SECONDS BEFORE I DRAG YOU DOWN THE STAIRS MYSELF SUTTON!"

Silently cursing her mother-in-law, Connie released her husbands behind so he could step away from her.

"She actually did that once," Xander said, "so we mustn't dawdle."

As Connie made to turn towards the stairs, she felt her husband's hand softly grasp her arm and she turned back to his intense gaze.

"May I come to your bed tonight?" Although she was certain he knew the answer, there still appeared to be some faint scepticism in his eyes.

Rising on her toes, Connie allowed her lips to hover an inch from his as she answered. "Only on the condition that I can kiss any part of you I wish to." She pressed a brief kiss on his lips as a low growl came from his throat.

Turning away from him, Connie walked to the top of the stairs where she looked down to see the Dowager Countess with her arms crossed and lips pursed in impatience.

Looking back, she observed her husband jog to reach her side whereupon he took her hand to place in his arm as he escorted her down the stairs to their waiting carriage.

Chapter Thirteen

Xander decided that nothing would bring down his mood for the night, although his mother did try. As the three of them sat in the carriage on their way to the concert, he could not help noticing the tension between his wife and his mother.

As he expected, it did not take long to find out the cause of the tension.

"Well Sutton, I suppose you have heard how your wife plans to ruin my life's work?" the Dowager Countess announced.

Giving Connie's hand a squeeze, Xander answered, "And what are we referring to when we say your life's work exactly?" His mother looked incredulous at him.

"My beautiful rooms of course." She put her hand to her heart and appeared to attempt tears as she continued. "All those incandescent colours, the furniture, the art, all gone! Sacrificed to the altar of blandness." She followed her outburst by dramatically falling back onto her seat, closing her eyes, and raising her hand to her brow.

"Are you finished?" One eye opened and narrowed in on Xander. "I'm afraid your manipulations shan't be working in this instance, if Connie wants to change the rooms she can."

With a tut, his mother sat back and glared at the pair of them. "How could you allow such beautiful rooms to be altered so?"

"Mother, I haven't been in the drawing room for at least three years because it gives me headaches."

"If it makes any difference, I only said I wanted to change a few things. I never intended for a full-scale renovation to take place." Connie contributed.

Turning to his wife, Xander grinned impishly, "Connie, if you do not redecorate the entire house, I shall be most disappointed in you!" His mother feigned a sob in the background.

Connie leaned in to whisper, "I do not wish to cause trouble with your mother. As much as an overhaul is needed, I thought smaller changes would be better at first."

"I am afraid the size of the change matters not," Xander responded, "my mother is going to dig her heels in any way she can."

"Is she always this dramatic?" Connie stole a glance at the woman in question.

"Unfortunately, yes. She managed to get her way in practically everything in her marriage by simply annoying my father." Leaning further in, Xander's voice became husky, "Do not attempt to emulate her though, I'll show you later how to get me to do anything you want." Xander was rewarded by a blush creeping across Connie's cheeks as she stifled a giggle.

"What are the two of you whispering about?" The pair turned to see the Dowager Countess observing them through narrowed eyes.

"Your son was just advising on what would please him the most." Connie said innocently.

His mother pursed her lips and proceeded to stare out of the carriage window. Seeing that his mother was determined to ignore them, Xander opted to softly stroke his wife's hand as he leant towards her again.

"If you really want to know what would please me, I can say you will need to have sturdy knees."

Connie looked at him with a bemused face and opened her mouth to respond.

"Oh look, we have arrived." Xander announced, enjoying the prospect of enlightening the woman later.

He helped both his wife and mother out of the carriage and escorted them both into Hatley House, the March's Kensington townhouse, where they greeted their hosts.

After the obligatory introduction, his mother soon disappeared to no doubt commiserate with her fellow witches and Xander escorted his wife into the reception room, where he could see several rows of seats arranged facing a pianoforte.

"What is it exactly we're watching tonight?" he enquired.

"There is going to be a performance by Angelica Catalani, I believe." Xander halted at his wife's words. "And how did one of the most popular opera singers in the world end up agreeing to perform a small concert hosted in the house of a viscount?"

"She and Viscountess March share a passion for their works for the poor. It is quite clever really; I have seen them pair up before. First Miss Catalani sings tragic pieces, building up the emotion of the guests. Then once she is finished, the Viscountess will appear to tell us of the plight of the poor, feeding on our already vulnerable state. Typically, this results in several guests pledging to donate, guilting others in contributing and then when the Viscountess calls on them the next day, they are forced to pay lest they be publicly shamed."

"And I suppose I shall be making a large donation?"

"Well, it would not do well for one of the ladies who collects the funds to have a husband refusing to donate now would it?" Connie teased.

Seeing Xander's confused look she explained, "One of my dearest friends is Viscountess March's daughter, Rachel.

We often get roped into her schemes, not that I complain about it. So, I shall be up early tomorrow to go collecting."

"I think you shall be too tired to do anything tomorrow." Xander muttered.

Connie's head whipped round to face his, "Did you say something?"

"I said we should take our seats." Xander could tell by her expression that Connie did not believe him. He ignored her questioning gaze as he led her to the middle of the back row.

"Why are we sitting here? There are several empty seats closer to the front?" she queried.

"Apparently I am already donating so the fellows who need more convincing shall be sat ahead." Xander explained, "Besides, I always enjoy sitting at the back. You'd be surprised what you can learn from watching the backs of people's heads."

Rolling her eyes, Connie said "In that case be sure to give me a full report on what you have learnt once the concert is over."

Before Xander could respond, he was shoved forward by a massive thump to his back. Slamming down in the seat besides him was Liam Ainsworth. Looking past him, Xander was confused to see his friend was alone.

"Is your family sick of you then?"

Before Liam could answer, a booming voice came from his other side.

"Showing off your wife tonight are you, Sutton?" Xander turned to see the tall form of Geoffrey Ainsworth, Duke of Bristol slink into the seat next to Connie's. Greeting the older man, he saw Connie stiffen out of the corner of his eye.

"It's good to see you, Your Grace. It was a shame you could not have attended the wedding."

"My apologies, son, I have a prior engagement I could not break." Turning to Connie, the Duke continued, "I did hear that you looked beautiful, Countess."

Connie uttered a timid thanks as she appeared to shrink under his gaze. Xander considered why his wife would appear so uncomfortable next to the man. Reflecting back, Xander had forgotten that Connie belonged to a family that would have sheltered her to have few encounters with the rival clan. No wonder she was so uncomfortable.

Taking his wife's hand in his, Xander put it in his mind to reassure her that the family would be warm and welcoming to her. Unfortunately, in this instance it was not helped by the Duke leaning over her as he spoke to him.

"We have excellent news to impart. I have a grandson!" The man boasted, shocking Xander.

"Was Colette not due to give birth for another month? Are she and the child well?"

"Healthy and strong, the both of them." That was a relief, Xander knew how much Colette worried about the birth.

"I assume they were not able to travel to Kent as planned then?"

"They will be going," Liam interjected, "but they will wait until a few weeks later than the original plan."

Before they could continue, Viscountess March began to address the room, presenting Miss Catalani. Soon the entire room was held in rapture by the singer.

Xander was unable to concentrate on the performance, however, as Connie's grip on his hand grew tighter. Stealing a glance at his wife, he saw she was wide-eyed, staring straight ahead and seeming to be trembling in fear.

Looking back to the front, Xander realised he had no idea what the Wexford family said about the Ainsworth's behind closed doors. Liam had tried to build bridges with the rival clan, but his attempts never resulted in any change.

He resolved to speak to her later to reassure her that he was practically a member of their family and had never witnessed anything untoward.

The performance eventually drew to a close, to rapturous applause naturally. Then just like Connie predicted, Viscountess March returned to the stage to ask for donations for the poor. Surprisingly, Xander found that her skills at speechmaking made the audience (and himself) just as emotional as Miss Catalina's performance and soon there were cheers of donations.

The second the crowd began to disperse, Connie excused herself citing the need to freshen up. The three men stared after her as she hurried away, and Liam whispered to Xander with a grin that he could not wait for the day when Xander and Connie would be dining with his family.

"I feel that day may be a while away." Was Xander's response.

It took several minutes for Connie to stop herself shaking. Sat in the ladies dressing room pretending to mend a button on her glove, she took several deep breaths and somehow managed to calm herself.

Tonight, was the first time, Connie realised, that she had ever been in close proximity with the devil that was the Duke of Bristol and Connie was terrified. Even more worrying was the knowledge that this could quite possibly become a regular occurrence. After all, she was now married to one of the closest friends of the future Duke and as a result would have no choice but to invite all members of the Ainsworth family to any events she hosted. Not to mention more intimate occasions.

"Constance Wexford! What are you doing hiding away in here?" Connie looked up to see the angelic face of Rachel March reflected in the mirror before her. She felt a rush of relief sweep over her for the distraction.

Her mouth lifted to a grin as she turned to her friend, "That's Constance Chalmers to you now."

"Oh yes," Rachel nudged Connie over to share her seat, "although you'll forgive me for not realising. After all, I was not invited to the wedding nor the wedding breakfast, was I?"

Connie blanched upon hearing the chastising, "You know I would have invited you had it not been so sudden, Rachel, but if it is any consolation, we did decide not to have a wedding breakfast so it would have been rather awkward had you arrived for it."

Rachel clearly suppressed a smile as she pretended to consider Connie's explanation. Connie decided to sweeten her friend further, "I suppose if I were to ask you to be the godmother to our firstborn child it would be incentive for you to forgive me?"

"Change it to firstborn son and I will never speak of the slight again." Connie nodded in ascent before grasping her friend's hands.

"There is so much I need to tell you."

"Yes, but first I need to know one thing," Rachel said, "are you happy?"

A soft smile graced Connie's lips as she answered, "Surprisingly, yes. Although I believe I shall be much happier once I go home."

Rachel's eyebrows rose in amusement. "Well, the sooner we take the required turns about the room the sooner we can make your wishes come true."

As the pair rose and left the dressing room arm in arm, Rachel continued, "When we go on our collecting journey tomorrow you shall have to give me all the details on *married life.*"

"I very much doubt there is much I can tell you that you have not bribed out of your sisters."

"I suppose not on that count," Rachel said, "but perhaps you could tell me how you managed to obtain two exceedingly serious marriage prospects in the space of two months."

By accidentally tricking one into ruining me.

Connie felt the familiar sting of regret that she should have forced Xander into marriage. No matter how well the marriage may turn out to be, she could not change that fact and would have to live with the guilt.

Her guilt would not be helped as the pair ventured into the reception room and were immediately confronted with the sight of an attractive woman of about thirty reaching to Xander in conversation and stroking his arm.

Rachel quickly sought to reassure her friend. "Have no worries where that one is concerned. Lady Walker does not hold a candle to you and the Earl would be a fool to entertain her attempts."

"Lady Walker?" Connie could not place the name.

"She is the wife of Sir Michael Walker, the poet." Her companion rolled her eyes, "His writings often bemoan how the young are foolish and have no consideration for their elders. So naturally he married a woman twenty years his junior."

That struck familiar to Connie, "Oh I remember now, Sir Michael was a guest at a dinner my parents hosted. Rather self-important I thought."

"I believe Lady Walker is close friends with your mother-in-law."

Connie laughed, "Anyone who willingly spends their time with my mother-in-law is someone to be avoided."

Rachel furrowed her brow at her words. "Perhaps married life is not entirely sunshine and roses."

"Oh, just wait until tomorrow, I believe she is the most confounding character I have ever come across."

"And who might that be?" The pair started before turning to see Connie's husband stood before them with a smile on his face.

"No-one." Both girls spoke in unison in voices far higher pitched than usual. Xander's eyes narrowed but he chose not to pursue the topic any further. Instead, he chose to bow his head towards Rachel.

"Alexander Chalmers, at your service My Lady." Connie did not miss the blush that graced her friend's cheeks as she curtsied in response.

"Rachel March, My Lord. I do hope you have been enjoying yourself this evening."

"Very much so, you must pass my thanks to your parents on my behalf." Xander turned to Connie as Rachel nodded in assent. "My apologies, darling, but would you consider cutting our evening short? I know you will need to wake early to go collecting." *And I wish to warm your bed as soon as possible* his eyes said.

Sharing a meaningful look with her friend, Connie and Xander made their goodbyes before making their way out to the carriage.

Biting her lip, Connie tried to quell the butterflies in her stomach in anticipation of what awaited her once they arrived home.

Chapter Fourteen

Anticipation exuded through Connie during the carriage ride home. Once they had arrived, Xander stopped her at the bottom of the stairs to tell her to go ahead to her room and wait for him there.

And so, Connie was sat at her dressing table, examining her appearance for any flaws in order to distract her from her nerves. The memory of their previous encounter drifted through her mind and Connie clenched her thighs together in the hopes of stilling the desire coursing through her.

Xander finally entered the room and his eyes met Connie's in the mirror's reflection. He had removed his coat and cravat and she counted five undone buttons on his shirt, allowing her to glimpse a hint of the hair speckled across his chest.

When she made to stand up, he held his hand up and requested that she stay exactly where she was. A tinge of worry broke through in her mind that her husband had decided he did not wish to share her bed after all. Staring at his reflection, Connie waited for his next move. All that could be heard was the crackles of the fireplace and the light sound of their breathing.

His deep voice broke through the silence, "I think before anything should happen, you and I need to ensure we are on the same page."

Connie pursed her lips and nodded as he continued, "I feel that you and I both know we can make this marriage a success and this feeling between us, whatever it may be, is strong. So, we should be much happier if we should give in rather than fight it."

She did not answer him as she wondered where he was leading to. Surely, they had already decided to give in to the attractions between them.

"But regardless of what lies in our future, I cannot in good conscience continue until I apologise for what I have done in the past." He leaned against the bedpost and nervously rubbed his hands together as he went on. "I cannot imagine how violated I must have made you feel."

"Violated?" Connie interrupted, "Why on earth should I feel violated?"

"Well, it was not me whom you invited to be with you that night," he answered. "You were under the impression that you had given your maidenhead to your fiancé, and now you have been forced to marry a man you do not know because I allowed myself to violate you without even finding out who you were."

Connie was stunned, they both shared the same guilt believing they had tricked the other into their current situation.

"It is I who should apologise to you!" Connie was exasperated, "You only went to the gallery because I had invited you, I clearly stated that I wanted you and I did not ask you to stop. In fact, being engaged I was clearly prepared to be married. Most men do not marry until they are at least a decade older than yourself therefore I most definitely have trapped you."

Xander looked to the ceiling in frustration, "Regardless of marriage, you believed you were giving yourself to another man and I took that awa........."

"I did not give myself to another man, Xander, I gave myself to you." Connie refused to allow him to say any more. "I had planned to invite Ernest to a secret rendezvous because I knew he would not even attempt to kiss me until the wedding day. I had not intended for anything further to happen."

Her voice softened as she stared into his eyes, "I may have thought you were another man but the only reason I gave my body was because it was to you. No one else could have made me feel the way I did that night....no one else could make me feel the way I do tonight."

She could feel her heartbeat in her throat as she waited for his response.

"Then I suppose it is time we stop arguing."

Connie's chest began to heave as she watched him stalk towards her. He stopped behind her and began to gently remove the pins from her coiffured hair, releasing the curled tendrils. She could no longer see his face in the mirror, but Connie did not fail to notice that a bulge had appeared in his trousers. Should she turn her head she would find herself with it directly in front of her face.

Xander ran his hand through her now-free tresses before reaching for hers and guiding her to stand.

Lifting her face to gaze at him, Connie shivered at the burning passion she saw in his eyes. As he leaned forward her eyes gently fluttered shut in readiness to meet his lips with hers.

Instead of the hard kiss she expected, Xander planted a brief soft kiss on her lips before moving his along her jaw to her ear, where he nipped her earlobe. His mouth then began a trail downward until he found a sensitive spot where her neck and shoulders met and promptly sucked.

Connie gasped as the sensation shot straight to her pelvis. She reached her hands up to run through his hair and hold him in place. A low laugh came from him and the resulting vibrations weakened Connie's knees.

Lifting his head, Xander gave Connie a wink as he removed one of her hands from his hair. Never breaking the shared gaze between them, he began undoing the buttons of her glove. Once all of them were loose, he slowly removed the glove from her arm, kissing each piece of skin as it was exposed. After dropping the glove to the floor, he repeated the process on her other hand.

Once both gloves were disposed of, he turned her and began to work on the buttons of her gown. As with her arms, he placed gentle kisses upon each area of skin that was exposed, and Connie shivered as she felt the dress pool at her feet.

Connie could not decide whether it was fortunate or unfortunate that the removal of her petticoat and stays did not expose any more of her body, as it meant that she would have a brief reprise from his torturous kisses.

The relief was short-lived, however, as Xander began to bunch up the skirt of her chemise and lift the entire item over her head. Her nipples tightened as they met with the air of the room and the coolness caused Connie to feel the moisture that was gathering in her crotch.

Continuing his gentle ministrations, Xander began to lightly knead her buttocks and Connie bit down a moan as the tension coiled in her.

He moved his hands to her hips to gently urge her to turn once again. For several silent moments, Connie could do nothing but stare at his face as he gazed along her naked body. The silence was finally broken when he growled just one word to reveal his view, "Perfection."

Connie tried to mask her smile at his appraisal, pleased that her husband should find her so appealing. Any semblance of a smile was lost, however, as he bent and resumed his trail of kisses, this time along her collarbone.

His fingertips lightly traced the sides and underside of her breasts as his lips travelled down to meet them. Goosebumps rose in the wake of his fingers as she rubbed her thighs together in frustration, needing him to do more.

Connie's head fell back, and she loudly moaned as his mouth finally took one of her breasts, suckling her as he cupped the other with his hand. His tongue began to flick her nipple as his fingers mirrored the actions on the other breast, causing Connie to cry out. She ran her hands through his hair as he alternated between breasts.

After several moments of torture, Xander lifted his head, his eyes glistening, as he lowered to his knees and ran his hands over her calves.

Lifting one leg, he removed her slipper and deliberately rolled down her garter and stocking, resuming his task of placing kisses upon each area of exposed skin. Returning her foot to the floor, he repeated the action on her other leg but instead concluded by resting her foot on the stool she had been sat on moments ago.

Connie became conscious of his stare as it fixed on her folds. She could feel the moisture pool further and silently willed him to take her in desperation. She did not think she needed anything more in that moment.

His head drifted until he began planting kisses over the inside of her thighs. Keeping one hand on her raised leg, he then moved the other to lightly trace through her folds. The sensation jolted through her as Connie's breathing grew heavier.

"Now this is the most beautiful flower in all existence." Xander said before raising his eyes to meet her gaze. "I'm going to worship you, Constance, is that alright?"

Connie's need for him was insatiable as she answered, *"Oh god, please!"*

He chuckled as he spread her folds with his fingers before leaning in and licking her.

"Oh, that is something.......that can be done?" Connie breathlessly worded.

His deep laugh vibrated through her body as he continued to devour her, choosing to leave her question unanswered.

Connie could only moan as he pleasured her. Her moans grew louder and louder and his actions quickened. With no warning, he pushed two of his fingers inside her, hitting spots inside her that made her gasp and writhe in pleasure.

The tension built up in her as she began to rock her pelvis into his face, prompting him to utter encouragements to move faster.

Pleasure grew as the need to topple over an edge she could not see heightened. Xander planted his lips upon the spot which seemed to be the root of the pleasure and began to suck. In that instant Connie finally toppled over the edge and screamed as she continued to ride his face in the hopes of prolonging it.

As Connie came down from her high, panting to regain her breath, she felt her legs weaken and would have collapsed had Xander not risen and put his arm around her back to hold her up. His other hand cupped her face as he took her mouth in a hard kiss, tongues clashed as he sought to dominate her. Connie moaned into his mouth as she tasted herself on him.

Regaining her senses, Connie found herself desperate for more and began to frantically tug at the buttons of his shirt in an attempt to release them. Giving up her attempts, she tugged at the clothing, sending buttons scattering across the floor as she greedily explored the firm lines of his chest with her hands.

Lowering his hands to her behind, Xander lifted her from the floor and moved until Connie found herself being pushed onto the bed.

Lying on her back, Connie watched her husband remove his clothing, her hips rising and falling in need as each inch of him was exposed to her.

When he finally stood before her tall and naked, Connie groaned at the sight of his thick manhood. Biting her lip, the memory of how it had felt pounding into her coursed through her. Rising onto her hands and knees, Connie crawled to the edge of the bed to take it in her hands.

She heard Xander's breath hitch as she explored the shape of him, cupping the flesh beneath and gently stroking him as he grew ever harder beneath her fingertips.

Lifting her eyes to meet his hooded gaze, Connie began to trail kisses along his chest, flicking her tongue over his nipple and placing light bites along the hard ridges of his stomach as her head inched lower and lower, determined to pay back the pleasure he had just given her.

When Connie was inches away from taking his cock in her mouth, however, Connie felt Xander's hands on her head as he gently lifted it away from his body.

"Not this time, flower." His voice was strained as he spoke, "As much as I want that, I need to be between your legs more."

He chucked as she whined in response, "We have all the time in the world, sweetheart, now lie back."

All prior thoughts vanished from her mind as Connie rested her head on the pillow and planted her feet wide, ready to welcome her husband into her.

Lowering himself on top of her, Xander gave Connie a slow, languid kiss. Resting an elbow by her head, his other hand travelled down to take hold of his cock and trace it along the folds of her womanhood, making Connie purr in pleasure.

Xander then positioned himself and unhurriedly push himself into her. Gasping at how filled she was, Connie stroked her hands over her husbands back as she beckoned him to wait.

Xander lavished attention upon her breasts as he waited for her to relax underneath him. As the pleasures of his mouth shot down to her pelvis, Connie began to unconsciously lift her hips to take more of him in.

Starting at a slow pace, Xander gently thrust in and out of her, going deeper with each movement until Connie had finally been able to take him in to the hilt.

As he began to gradually build up speed, Connie felt the familiar coil of tension spring through her as the pleasure began to rise. Clinging to him, she wrapped her legs around his hips, bringing him in deeper and frantically meeting his thrusts with her own as her moans grew louder.

Once again finding herself on the precipice, Connie's eyes screwed shut as she chased her release. Sensing her need, Xander took her hand and brought it to where to two were joined.

Leaning over her, he licked the beads of moisture on her cheek before speaking, "Find that little nub I touched earlier and rub circles on it."

Heeding his orders, Connie began to rub circles and felt her pleasure increase. Spurred on by the sounds of his grunting, Connie pressed harder in time with his thrusts until his cock slammed against one particular point and she began screaming as her release came.

Lifting himself off her, Xander rose to his knees, taking her hips in his hands and pounding harder than before, making her release even stronger.

As she finally began to come down from her high, Xander gave one final thrust and she felt him shudder and release inside her.

Holding her still for a moment, he pulled himself out and collapsed onto his side. The air was filled by the heat of their lovemaking and the pair's pants filled the room as they struggled to regain normal breathing.

For what felt like an eternity they just lay in an L-shape, catching their breath and basking in the afterglow of their passion. As she regained control of her senses, a million thoughts whisked through Connie's mind over what would happen next for the pair. Opting to approach the subject in a cautious manner, she broke the silence.

"What normally happens next?" Out of the corner of her eye she saw him lift his head to look at her. "I mean, after the *act*, what do we do now?"

Xander crawled up the bed to lie on his side facing her. Turning onto hers to meet his gaze, Connie felt his hand lightly stroke her face.

"Whatever we wish to do, flower." He softly smiled at her as he spoke. "We could talk, bathe, eat......there is no right or wrong. What do you wish to do?"

Connie furrowed her brow as she considered her answer. Looking to him, she spoke hopefully.

"Could we do it again?"

A flicker of surprise crossed his features before lust overtook them. With a growl, Xander pounced on top of her, bringing Connie to rapturous giggles before turning them to moans.

Chapter Fifteen

The next two weeks passed by in utter bliss for Xander. Every time the opportunity presented itself, he found himself pulling Connie into an intimate embrace. Embraces that soon turned salacious to the point where his wife, on one occasion, had to drag him into a more private room lest the servants catch them making love against a wall in the hallway.

What surprised him the most, however, was how much he found himself enjoying his wife's company outside of the carnal activities. When they were out in society, be it at a ball, garden party or art exhibition, he found himself in awe at how she eased through any social situation they found themselves in. Indeed, she had yet to make any faux pas in public.

Meanwhile, Xander found himself at the most ease he had ever been in his own home. Never had he found simply reading in silence in another's presence so soothing. He grew impressed at how pragmatic Connie was when taking charge of the renovations of the house. He found himself laughing as they played cards after dinner, softly singing to himself as they both dressed for the day and avoiding leaving his bed until the very last moment so he could watch her as she woke.

Naturally, he found himself the butt of his friend's jokes as they mocked how eager he was to return home following every jaunt or meeting. Xander made a mental note to pay them all back in kind when they found themselves in married bliss.

Following one particular meeting at Boodles, Xander returned home to find the house in utter chaos. Workmen were wandering all around and one could not move without risking tripping over debris. Startled by the sight that greeted him, Xander searched the house for his wife, eventually finding her in the drawing room.

Sneaking up on her as she extolled the workers as they pasted the paper-hangings onto the walls. He earned a gasp from Connie as he grasped her hips and kissed her neck.

"Alexander Chalmers," she said in a hushed tone, "I have no wish to take part in a sordid exhibition for the workmen!"

Xander chuckled as he turned her to face him in his arms, "If you have no wish to become an exhibitionist, my flower, then you must drag me to our bedroom before I lift your skirts and take you against one of these freshly-pasted walls." He was pleased to see a blush rise in her cheeks.

"And do my freshly-pasted walls please you?" She rose her eyebrows in a challenge.

"They are my favourite shade of blue."

"The walls are green, darling. You would notice if you actually looked at them."

"I do not need to look at the walls to know you have chosen an exquisite colour for them." He still did not take his eyes off her. "Just as I know the furniture will be exquisite. Just as I know the art shall be exquisite."

"I sense a theme forming or do you not know any more adjectives?" His hands began rubbing her back as he pulled her in closer to align his mouth with her ear.

"In all honestly I have suddenly found myself lost for words." He whispered.

"And why might that be?" She answered, breathlessly.

"After saying I wished to lift your skirts that is now the only thing I am able to think of at this moment." He paused for effect before continuing. "In fact, your blushing has made my thoughts even more sordid. I find myself needing to strip you bare and kiss every inch of skin that it reaches."

He was pleased to hear a small squeak emerge from her mouth as she took in his meaning and uttered under her breath something about having "a betraying Gaelic complexion."

Before he could further torture his wife, a throat cleared to his left and their heads turned to the source of the sound. Connie pushed herself out of his arms as she introduced Xander to the chief workman, Mr Farlow.

"Pardon my interruption Milord," he then returned his gaze to Connie as he sought to explain himself, "Milady, you see we're readying all the pieces you do not wish to keep so we can transport them to the auction house."

Confusion crossed Connie's features, "Yes, that is what I asked to be done. Has there been any problems with the pieces?"

"Well, that's just it, Milady," the man rubbed the back of his neck as he went on, "the pieces are disappearing."

Xander was astounded. "How can pieces be disappearing? If I find out that your men are taking them…....."

"No, not my men, Milord." The man hastily interrupted, "it's yours who are taking them."

Gaping at the nerve of the man, Xander found himself struggling to keep his anger in check. "Are you insinuating that members of my household, whom I pay above average wages to might I add, are so brazenly stealing from me?"

Placing a hand on his arm, Connie sought to ease the tension by gently taking over the questioning.

"Please forgive my husband for his shock, Mr Farlow, but I am also perplexed as to what exactly is happening. What exactly are the servants doing?"

Farlow shuffled awkwardly, "They're taking the pieces upstairs Milady. One of my lads kept watch and said they were all going to the same room."

"Which room?"

"If I remember correctly," he twisted his mouth as he recollected, "he said he turned right at the top of the stairs and it was the fifth door on the left."

Xander and Connie both groaned as they realised which room he was referring to. Xander thanked the man and said he would take care of the situation.

Once Farlow had left, Connie turned back to her husband and sighed, "What are we going to do?"

Xander grasped her arms and kissed her forehead before answering, "You, flower, are not going to do anything. I on the other hand am going to walk upstairs and straighten it all out."

"Are you sure you do not need my help?" Xander rested his forehead against hers and closed his eyes, saying a silent prayer for some kind of divine intervention.

"Unfortunately, I feel if you come with me, it will just aggravate her more." Lifting his head, Xander let out a breath. "No, I shall have words with my mother. She cannot keep this up much longer."

Lifting onto her toes, Connie placed a light kiss on his lips and wished him luck before turning to continue her supervisions.

Dragging his feet, Xander walked the distance until he was stood in front of the entrance to his mother's rooms.

Cracking his knuckles in preparation, he sought the confidence he needed before knocking on the door to the viper's nest.

"Enter." Xander wondered if his mother's shrill tones would ever stop giving him the shivers.

The door did not open halfway when Xander found something appeared to block it from the other side. Peering around the door, he saw that the blockage came from lime-green footstool.

Squeezing through the gap in the doorway, Xander saw that the footstool was not the only object cluttering the floor. In fact, he was unable to see any carpet at all. Peering about the room, he saw his mother sat on a chaise-lounge next to the room's bay window and so began to haphazardly navigate his way across the room, climbing over several pieces of furniture and breaking at least one vase in the process.

Collapsing onto the other side of the settee, he cast his mother a disbelieving look before uttering a single word: "Why?"

Opting to focus on her needlework rather than looking at her son, the Dowager Countess took several seconds before responding. "Now Sutton, you and I both know I raised you better than to both refuse to greet your mother in deference and to not articulate your questions correctly."

"My apologies mother, allow to start again." His eyes narrowed at the way her lips titled in smug satisfaction. "Good day, you old bat, what on earth has possessed you to hoard our soon to be former belongings."

Her head shot up in attention, eyes blazing at his rudeness. "How dare you speak to your mother that way! I am one and forty, that does not constitute as old."

"Most women are considered to be on the shelf by the time they are five and twenty."

"Well luckily for me, I made a great marriage for myself before I reached that age and so was able to retain my youthful complexion."

"I shall pretend that your words make sense." Xander rolled his eyes at her vanity. "Shall we discuss the elephant in the room already? I have no desire to spend any time in your poisonous presence than necessary."

"Poisonous, am I? You never spoke to me in such a way before you married." She tapped her chin with her finger as she feigned contemplation. "I wonder what has caused this insolence?"

"Will you please stop avoiding the question and answer me?"

"Why have I rescued these beautiful pieces of art from your callous abandonment?" Xander slouched back as he readied himself for the onslaught. "You may have allowed your little chit to destroy the décor I have spent over twenty years perfecting but I do not have to allow the pieces I personally selected to leave the family."

A twinge of guilt crossed over Xander as he realised how much he had displaced his mother in the space of a few weeks. The guilt soon disappeared as she continued.

"I feel you are being a little too obvious of course. Suddenly obtaining a backbone when you have a wife to stroke your ego. And what will happen to you when she shows her true colours?"

Xander clenched his fist and dug his nails into his skin to distract him from his anger.

"After all, she shall just be continuing her family's legacy. One older brother is a cuckold, another larking around bedding all the married ladies of the Ton and that's not to mention the youngest Wexford brat, we all know how he almost killed the Prince of Wales."

"Mother, almost dousing a man in syrup does not equate with attempted manslaughter." The Dowager Countess waved her hand in dismissal.

"The point is, Sutton, that the girl will soon grow tired of you and seek company elsewhere. She has already done it once! Sir Ernest Fawcett had a lucky escape if you ask me."

Xander rubbed his hands over his face as he refused to entertain her tirade any longer. "It is no use continuing your hateful rants, mother! They will only lead you into further disfavour. Need I remind you that I told Connie to change everything only after you reacted to her minor suggestions in such an ugly manner."

"Well, she made such ugly suggestions."

"I do not care, mother, Connie is my wife, and you need to accept her as such. You are no longer the only woman in this household, and you need to stop throwing all of your toys out of the pram and behave in a respectable fashion."

His mother's nostrils flared in defiance as she listened to his words. Instead of fulfilling his expectations and answering back with some kind of snide remark, she chose to turn her face down to resume her needlework and said no more.

Searching her face for any sign of response, Xander understood that any attempts of further conversation were futile.

Standing up, he navigated his way back to the door. Pausing, with his hand on the doorknob, Xander turned his head back to make one final endeavour.

"Please consider, for the sake of both our happiness, allowing yourself to exhibit some form of kindness." Silence followed and Xander left the room.

Resting against the door once he closed it behind him, Xander closed his eyes and shut out the din echoing through the house.

It appeared the newlywed bliss would soon come to a crashing halt as his mother sought to disrupt any happiness he would have.

Unfortunately, it seemed to open a hole that had harboured all the conflicts he had pushed to the back of his mind in blissful ignorance. Conflicts that he knew would put he and his wife at odds.

In truth, Xander had willingly postponed discussing developing a relationship with the Ainsworth family with Connie. She would not greet the prospect warmly and he would need to gather all the weapons in his arsenal to show her that they were kind and good people. Perhaps it would also help him in discovering what exactly was preventing the Wexford's from reaching any sort of a resolution to this ridiculous feud.

It struck Xander then that should he not be able to resolve these tensions, he risked alienating all the people in his life to make Connie happy. And when it came to choosing between his wife and his loved ones, he was not sure exactly what choice he would make.

Chapter Sixteen

As much as she was enjoying her new life with her husband, managing her own home, and overseeing the renovations of the house, Connie could not deny that sitting in the parlour of her childhood home, surrounded by the family after an informal family meal made her feel a sense of comfort and ease she had yet to fully obtain in her marital home.

Sat with her mother and Jane, she was thrilled to observe how well Xander was fitting in with her family. Indeed, he was currently stood with her father and brothers, engaged in an animated discussion regarding the recent passing of a Daniel Lambert, debating how he had managed to achieve the unenviable title of 'fattest man in Britain'.

Connie pleasure grew even greater as Duncan turned to meet her eyes and gave a subtle nod, indicating that her husband had obtained the approval of at least one brother.

Smiling to herself, she returned her attention to the conversation between the ladies. Jane had been particularly interested in the progress of the redecoration.

"I must say, after visiting on Tuesday, I found myself exceedingly jealous of the quality of the upholstery you selected." Jane wistfully said. "As a matter of fact, once Matthew returned home that evening, he immediately found himself cornered as I attempted to convince him to allow for renovations of our own home."

Cora took a sip of her wine before asking, "And how well did your attempts go?"

"Terribly," Jane pouted, "he quickly began to lecture me that it was a waste of money that we could not justify paying."

"Unfortunately for you, my dear Jane, you have had the misfortune of marrying the most frugal of my brothers."

Jane huffed in response, "Marry the heir to a dukedom my mother said, you shall have all that you desire." Mischievously flicking her eyes between the two women, she added, "Every occasion in which the opportunity presents itself, I make sure to remind her of her words."

Connie placed her hand over her mouth to stifle her giggles. Cora, on the other hand, bore a frustrated look as she vented her thoughts. "Try as I may, I cannot understand how I managed to raise such a foolish son. And that is using kind words!"

Reaching over to take her mother-in-law's hands, Jane soothed her. "Do not be angry on my behalf. I achieve my revenge in small tortures that he has no clue are intentional."

She paused before turning back to Connie, "But we are not discussing my troubles now. Connie, dearest, are the workers causing any trouble? I know they can sometimes be a nuisance."

"Not the workers," Connie frowned. She looked up to observe two curious faces looking at her curiously, prompting further explanation. "Xander's mother is being rather.........unhelpful."

"What do you mean when you say unhelpful, darling?" Connie's mother asked.

"She has been unwelcoming to the prospect of change and then when confronted with the fact that she is not going to get her own way she bursts into the most outlandish theatrics that leave me gobsmacked. Not to mention her little schemes to undermine my authority."

Jane appeared to consider her thoughts before delicately responding, "Can I ask, Connie, how you approached the Dowager Countess with your changes. You are conducting quite an overhaul after all."

"I did try to be pragmatic at first, but her reaction showed me that I would not win no matter my attempts."

"Surely the woman cannot be that stubborn." Cora contributed. "Stand your ground, Connie. If you give in now, she will believe she can do anything."

"Perhaps a peace offering would soothe her?" Connie's eyebrows rose at Jane's suggestion. Surely, she could see that nothing would appease the woman.

Seeming to sense Connie's apprehension, Jane explained her reasoning. "It is just that I do not know if you understand just how great this change is for her."

"How great a change?" Connie was incredulous. "I refuse to believe that she could be *that* affected by my presence in the house."

"I understand that she is being overdramatic dear, but I do not think she has ever had to deal with a situation such as this before."

"What situation? Being replaced?" Connie mused.

"Not replaced but no longer being the only woman in the home." Connie blinked in surprise at her sister-in-law's words. "If I remember correctly the previous Earl's mother passed away in childbirth, he had no brothers, and his sole uncle was unmarried. You are the first woman to marry into the family since the Dowager Countess and I imagine that must make her feel rather displaced."

"I did not consider that."

Jane softly laughed, "I was very lucky in that I married a man with several female relatives, I imagine it must be odd for her."

Connie looked to her mother, who appeared to consider Jane's theory. "I suppose that is possible. Perhaps you should give her a token of good will and then if she still behaves appallingly, we can say she is simply an *unpleasant* character." Cora crinkled her nose at the last part.

"She shall have to be warmer at some point, in any case, as she may have a grandchild on the way shortly." Jane sent Connie a challenging look, making the younger woman blush and look to her hands in her lap.

Eager to continue this change in conversation, Cora began to interrogate her daughter, "Is there perhaps any news in that regard?"

"Mother, your attempt at nonchalance is failing miserably." Connie chided.

"Oh, please just tell me, are you, or aren't you?" Connie could feel the two pairs of eyes burning into her as they anxiously awaited her response.

"I may be, but I cannot say for certain." Both women's faces lit up in joy at the prospect.

"I cannot tell you how wonderful it shall be to be a grandmother." Connie softened seeing the tears in her mother's eyes.

"I cannot wait to begin teasing the men over there about it. Duncan hates it when I know a secret he doesn't!" Jane joyfully announced, bringing out some light-hearted ire in Connie.

"Don't you dare!" she chided "I shall not be the cause of any mischief you have planned."

"Oh please," Jane laughed off, "should I remind you of your behaviour during my first year of marriage? You would not stop asking me if I was with child, often making your enquiries in the most public settings, to my horror."

Connie blanched at the reminder. Before she could respond, however, the trio were interrupted by the curious voice of her eldest brother, who was making his way across the room to them.

"What are you three lovely ladies discussing?"

"Why you have not provided me with a grandchild yet." Came his mother's chiding response. Without missing a step, Matt swerved around and returned to the men's conversation, causing the trio of women to burst into a gaggle of laughter.

As Connie and Xander were saying their goodbyes at the end of the evening, Connie was pleased at how well it had gone. Thinking back to her discussion with her mother and Jane, she decided that perhaps tonight she would tell her husband that they may be expecting a child, which she was certain he would be overjoyed to hear.

She was brought out of her musings when a hand appeared on her shoulder. Turning to see its owner, she saw her eldest brother directing a serious look to her.

"Do I have something on my face brother?" she said nervously. Matt nodded his head in the direction of the library in an unspoken request for an audience. Looking back to see the rest of her family distracted, Connie followed him into the room.

Softly closing the door behind her, Connie leant back an observed her brother, curiosity growing greater.

Perching himself against the edge of their father's desk, Matt rubbed his hand over his face, seeming unsure on how to proceed.

"Whatever it is you wish to speak to me about, brother, might I ask that you hurry? The carriage will be waiting."

"I must say I was unsure at first, but Sutton appears to be a pleasant sort and he makes you happy."

Connie's confusion grew further, "You have summoned me to advise you approve of my husband?"

Matt chortled at her bemusement, "There is one qualm I have with your husband, can you guess?"

Connie stared daggers at her brother, casually perched on the desk with his arms folded and an amused smile on his face.

"I imagine it is the same thing that has set the entire Ton's tongues wagging I am married to a man who is close friends with a family who we refuse to associate with."

"Connie," Matt began.

"Do not 'Connie' me, I am well aware that you wish me to stay away from them, but it cannot be avoided. Besides, I feel it is indicative of their character's that both Harry and I have developed a fondness for Lady Elizabeth from our few encounters with her."

Connie paid no heed as Matt's eyes widened in irritation, "Besides, you and I both know that if it were not for Lady Elizabeth, I would not be married and would most likely be facing the prospect of shaming the entire family with an illegitimate child!"

Matt ran his hands through his hair as he responded, "Constance I know some things cannot be avoided but you forget that you are my only sister, and I should be both heartbroken and guilt-ridden should anything happen to you!"

Connie was taken aback by her brother's outburst. She began to nervously fiddle with the ends of her sleeves as she took in exactly what her brother was implying.

Lifting her head to meet his gaze, Connie's eyes softened, and the corners of her mouth turned up in an attempt of a smile.

"I haven't forgotten, Matt."

"Please promise me you will be careful where that family is concerned," he implored, "they may appear friendly but you and I both know what they are capable of."

Connie felt her eyes water as she began to realise how much of a toll her marriage could potentially take.

"What if Xander does not accept that I do not wish to have any contact with them?"

Matt moved forward, enveloping his sister in his arms as he rested his chin upon her head. "Be thankful that yours is a marriage of circumstance and not love."

He carefully pushed his hands onto Connie's shoulders so he could look at her face. The look on his face reminded her of an occasion when she, as a small child, managed to separate from the rest of the family in the village near their family estate. Not realising she had wandered into the road; Connie had frozen upon seeing a horse and carriage charging towards her. Matt had then appeared out of nowhere, pulling her off the street. She had never forgotten the look of worry on his face that day, a look that was now showing once again.

"It's not so bad you know," he attempted a smile, "never allow your marriage to define who you are. There is a whole world out there waiting to see all that you can do."

Pressing a sliver of a kiss upon her hair, Matt made to leave the room. Connie was saddened by his words, wishing he and Jane had been able to make their marriage happy. In that moment she came to the realisation that, should quarrels also form between Connie and her husband, it would be the second marriage to be destroyed by the Ainsworth's in their family.

Not only that, but she had seen the way Harry had looked at Eliza Ainsworth and began to worry that his would be another heart broken by that family.

Channelling a steely resolve, Connie decided that the honeymoon period with her husband would need to come to an end.

Yes, when they returned home, she would tell him in no uncertain terms would she be open to a relationship of any sort with the Ainsworths. If he had any challenges to her decision, then it would be a hill she would die on.

Besides, it was as Matt had said, theirs was a marriage based on circumstance and there was no love between them.

At least that is what Connie told herself as she made her way back to her family.

Chapter Seventeen

Xander knew, without a doubt, that something was troubling his wife.

To the average onlooker, there was nothing amiss. The silence in the carriage ride home would have been seen as comfortable owing to Connie resting her head upon his shoulder and her hand on his arm. To Xander, however, her hand grasped his arm far tighter than it normally would and he could see her bite her lip out of the corner of his eye.

Their night-time routine upon returning home was no different either. They dismissed the servants who greeted them and proceeded to Connie's room where they undressed one another and made love.

On an ordinary night, the pair would bask in a post-lovemaking bliss, laughing about the happenings of the day and revealing their innermost thoughts to one another.

Xander lay on his back, with his head upon a pillow as his wife's head rested on one of her arms, which was draped across his chest. Looking down at her, he could see a wariness in her eyes and so he lifted his hand to cautiously stroke her hair.

The movement caused Connie to lift her eyes to meet his and her lips lifted in a slight smile as she gazed up at him.

"Penny for your thoughts." Xander spoke softly, not wishing to dispel the peace that encapsulated the room.

Connie furrowed her brow, clearly considering her words before she spoke, "Do you ever wish we could just run away?" Xander tilted his head in confusion. "I mean, escape from all the outside forces that threaten your happiness?"

Bemused at her sentiment, he prompted her, "Do you mean with society? Unfortunately, it's a sacrifice we must make: Wealth and opulence in exchange for gossipers who like nothing better than to see you fail."

Connie buried her head in his chest as she stifled a giggle. "I am being serious!" came the muffled reply.

In a flash, Xander rolled the pair over so that he his legs rested between hers and they came face to face.

"I will have you know, my delectable wife, that I am being completely serious." He accented each word with kisses over her face and neck.

"I simply mean that we have begun this marriage with far more obstacles than most do, and it is not entirely optimistic." She tried and failed to halt his kisses as she spoke.

Xander lifted his head and gave her a wicked grin, "You are absolutely correct, Constance. We have nothing to be positive about whatsoever!"

Connie narrowed her eyes, clearly seeing that he did not take her concerns seriously.

"If we must list them," Xander continued, "then what problems do we have? A frightful mother determined to cause trouble," he punctuated the point with a kiss on her neck. "A shockingly brief engagement following a non-existent courtship which has turned all the eyes of the entire Ton on us." He kissed the other side of her neck. "Being an older, less Italian version of Romeo and Juliet." He licked the shell of her ear, garnering a moan. "We knew practically nothing about one another when we wed." He nibbled her other ear.

He turned his head so that their lips were barely an inch apart. "I cannot speak for you, but I do not believe we have a single thing we should be hopeful about in this marriage." He finished by reaching down and holding his cock, slowly dragging it up and down her folds, eliciting a sharp intake of breath from the woman beneath him.

Before he could continue his teasing, Connie clasped her hand on the back of his neck and brought his head down to kiss her. Xander mirrored the languid strokes of his cock with his tongue, revelling in the eroticism of the kiss.

He lifted his head as he entered her, looking deep into her eyes. Thrusting in and out of her heat at a leisurely pace, Xander sought to reassure his wife.

"Whatever worries you have, whatever troubles we face, I will always choose you!" Overcome by the adoration in her eyes, Xander sped up his movements. "God Connie, I think I would die rather than not choose you."

Connie cried out his name as she met his quickening speed. Soon all words were lost to frantic kisses and moans as they grew more and more frantic in their lovemaking. Connie soon peaked and the clench of her sex around him caused him to immediately follow her.

It took some time before the pair could catch their breath, as they continued their desperate kisses, needing even more of one another.

Later, Xander listened to the even sounds of Connie's breathing as she slept, arms wrapped around his torso. His thoughts drifted in worry to what could have caused his wife's sudden uncertainty.

Indeed, he mused, they had spent the past month of marriage in bliss, ignorant to the outside world. Of course, Connie would be wary, after all, it was the women who suffer when societal expectations are not met. Could there have been a sly comment said to her concerning their marriage?

Whatever it was, Xander resolved to speak to Connie in the morning regarding it. He just needed to make sure they were both fully clothed lest he be distracted......again.

As is typical when one makes plans to resolve any problems, they are prevented from coming to fruition.

In this case, Xander's intentions to speak with his wife were stalled when she was summoned on a charitable errand by Viscountess March.

Irritated at what he saw as a clearly avoidable summons, he decided to visit Ainsworth House and apologise for his lack of social interaction of late.

He was pleased to find his adoptive family fully understanding, giving him the grace of a honeymoon period, even though the pair had not actually gone on a honeymoon. Naturally, this led Xander to decide that upon the completion of the house renovations, he would take his wife to the continent for a late honeymoon.

Even more pleasing, Xander found, was that the Ainsworth women were delightfully inquisitive about his wife. He was inundated with questions about her character and preferences, and the ladies gave every indication of wishing to welcome Connie into their family as they had done so for him.

In fact, when Xander left the house in the early afternoon, he took with him a basket of the famous Ainsworth chutney to give to Connie along with an invitation to dinner in two evenings time.

He returned home to be informed that his wife had yet to return home, but his mother was hosting her coven in the drawing room. No doubt taking claim to the redesign, Xander thought.

Xander stealthily made his way to his office, managing to avoid greeting his mother or her friends, and poured himself a brandy as he began to look over the figures that Calvert had sent over the previous day. Figures that Xander had set aside when his wife had chosen to come and distract him.

Smiling at the memory, Xander began to immerse himself in numbers for some time until he reached for his glass only to find it empty.

"Would you like me to fill your glass for you?" came a husky voice from the door. Xander lifted his head to see who had intruded into his sanctuary.

Bugger!

Staring back at him with a lustful look in her eyes was Lady Margaret Walker. Xander masked a grimace as he remembered several past occasions when they had met, and the woman had clearly indicated a wish for him to come to her bed.

If Xander had not been married and Lady Walker had not been a constant companion to his mother, indication of character enough, he would have taken her up on her offer. After all, with her dark hair, dazzling blue eyes, plump lips, and high cheekbones, she was truly a beautiful woman who any sane man would lust over.

Unfortunately for Lady Walker, Xander had happened to have found a wife ten years her junior who had just as much beauty as she did. Indeed, Xander realised that Connie actually bore quite a startling resemblance to the woman in front of him. A woman who, whilst he was lost in his musings, had now come to stand in front of his desk.

Leaning over the desk and showing a scandalous amount of cleavage in the process, Lady Walker reached out and took the glass from his hand, making sure to brush her fingertips against his as she did so.

Xander gave himself a light slap on his face as her back was turned to fill the glass and he cleared his throat to engage in conversation when she made her way back to the desk.

"As lovely as it is to be blessed with your company, Lady Walker, surely my mother will be wondering where you have gotten to." The sooner he got her to return to his mother's side, the better.

Rather than responding immediately, she lifted his glass to take a sip of the freshly poured brandy and made sure to run her tongue over her lips as she placed the glass in his hand. Xander inwardly groaned at the sight.

Why does she have to look so much like Connie?

Settling herself in the seat in front of his desk, she finally responded. "I have told you so many times, Xander, that you must call me Margaret." *And I never told you to call me Xander.* "But if you must know, I saw you sneaking in earlier and decided that I must come pay you a visit. I never get to see you on your own anymore." Her lips formed a sensual pout as she finished.

"I am afraid that is what happens when one becomes a married man. I suddenly find myself unwilling to spend my time with women other than my wife, no matter how," he paused as she slowly ran a finger up and down her neck, "enticing the woman in question."

Laughter swept the room as she listened to his words. "My dear Xander, surely you do not mean to insult my intelligence so?"

"And how have I done that may I ask?"

"A three-day engagement to a girl no one in society had ever paired your name with, come now it is rather obvious."

"Actually, you will find it was a four-day engagement and I had known Connie for at least a month before we became engaged."

"An entire month!" She raised her hand to her chest in mock surprise. "Now that indubitably changes things. Of course, now I believe that you came to your marriage fully acquainted with your wife and with no possible scandal attached at all."

Xander received a pointed look as Lady Walker made it noticeably clear that no one would be fooled by his attempts of amending the narrative.

"I should think it hardly matters how Connie and I came to be wed," he said, "we are married now and are incredibly happy together."

Lady Walker scoffed, "You are happy with that little girl? Come now, you can be honest with me."

"Connie is a married woman now and believe me when I say she is most pleasing to be married to." As seductive as the woman's body language was, she could no longer distract him from his annoyance at her dismissiveness towards his wife.

"And when the novelty wears off?"

"It won't."

"Xander, darling, there is no need to be so angry at me. I am just saying to your face what everyone else is behind you back."

"I do not care what is being said behind my back, Lady Walker, I only care for my wife's happiness."

With that Xander rose and made his way over to pull the insufferable woman from her seat. "I think we should end this conversation and have you returned to my mother!"

"Of course, I shall take my leave if you so wish it." She spoke nonchalantly as she smoothed the skirts of her sage dress. "But may I give you a word of advice?"

Xander struggled not to roll his eyes as he nodded in the hopes of this bringing the conversation to its end.

"You have opened the eyes of a young, impressionable girl to a world she has had no idea existed until now." She flicked a speck of dirt from his shirt. "And now she has had a taste of what is available, she will begin to wonder if a tastier dessert lies on someone else's table."

Xander scoffed in response.

"You may think I am being ridiculous, but it is true. When I married Michael, I did not even consider that I should prefer the company of other men but here I am now. Just as your mother was, just as your precious Duchess Ainsworth was, just as every woman in the Ton is. You are denying the inevitable and once you realise that the day has come, I hope you will remember this."

Xander was still reeling from the suggestion that Verity may have engaged in extramarital relations when lips crashed onto his. He froze in shock as he felt her tongue probe his mouth. He came to his senses, however, upon feeling a small hand firmly clasp him through his trousers and he lifted his hands to her shoulders to push her away.

As was the case with luck typically attributed to Xander, the second their lips parted a gasp was heard and his head whipped round to see his wife stood, wide-eyed in the doorway.

Before Xander could utter her name and start towards her, Connie quickly turned and fled the room.

"Well, I suppose that has quickened the proceedings." He turned with daggers in his eyes to the woman stood next to him.

"I have never in my life hit a woman," he fumed, "but if you do not leave this house in five seconds that will change."

With a smirk, Lady Walker silently sauntered out of the room, leaving Xander feeling angry, lost, and violated.

Chapter Eighteen

A bevy of emotions raged through Connie as she retreated to the garden in need of sanctuary. She held onto a column of the gazebo as she sought to catch her breath.

Try as hard as she might she could not erase the image of her husband in another woman's arms and tears began to well up as she processed the sting of his betrayal. How could he do this to her after the words he spoke to her the night before?

The thought gave Connie further pause. If Xander could so easily lie to her last night when else had he lied to her? Horror broke through as she realised how much of a fool she had been. Not only was he being both untruthful and unfaithful, but he was also most likely laughing at her behind her back. She could only imagine the way he was laughing with the Ainsworth's over how much of a fool the naïve Wexford girl had made of herself. Matt was right after all it seemed.

She resolved to allow the tears at his betrayal flow through now and once they had stopped, she would straighten her back, gather all her strength and never allow her husband the chance to hurt her ever again.

And if Connie could not be strong enough for herself, she would without a doubt be strong for the child she carried.

After what felt like an eternity, Connie wiped away the last of her tears and smoothed her skirts. Turning to return to the house, a small gasp escaped her throat as she saw her husband stood several feet away from her.

Gathering all her strength to attempt a steely resolve, Connie began the confrontation.

"How long have you been standing there?"

"Only a few minutes," his voice was hoarse, "I wanted to hold you, but I thought that would not be welcomed at this time."

"No, it would not." Connie said bitterly. Her anger grew as she observed how he struggled to meet her eyes and shuffled sheepishly, it appeared he thought to behave submissively in the hopes of obtaining her forgiveness, thinking her still a fool.

She marched up to him and jabbed a finger in his chest. "Did you and your lady lover laugh over how much of a fool you made of me?"

His eyes widened, "You think I welcomed those affections?"

"I watched you for several seconds kiss another woman and allowed her to…...you let her…...she had her hand upon you. In our own house, in the very room where one day ago you pushed me onto my knees and……"

"I did not invite her advances and was so in shock at her nerve that I did not push her away as soon as I should have." He interrupted her tearful accusations. "For that I apologise but I have done naught else wrong!"

Processing his words, Connie struggled to recall if he had been responding to the woman. She did not realise she had been chewing on her lip until she felt his thumb gently brush it. She turned her gaze upwards and almost jumped at the intensity of his stare.

He continued running his thumb along her lower lip as his hand cupped her jaw. She suddenly found herself short of breath and smothered a gasp when his head bent, and lips met her neck.

"Constance, my love," he whispered between kisses, "I don't want her…….....I have never wanted her……. never welcomed her kisses……I only want you." Her hands clenched into fists by her sides as she struggled to stop herself giving in to his entices.

His hands began exploring her body as he continued his denials. Every inch of Connie desperately wanted to believe him. She felt a war wage between her heart and head.

Her head sought to remind her that she was a pawn in his games, seeking to humiliate her for the amusement of him and his friends.

Her heart, meanwhile, pounded with the need to forgive and embrace the man she loved. She shivered at the realisation; she had fallen in love with her husband!

In any other circumstance, Connie would feel wonderful at the thought of being blessed with a marriage filled with such love but, rather than welcoming the emotion, it turned her even more cold to his advances.

Xander was practically a member of a family that had hurt her own, that callously ruined the lives of people she loved. If she allowed him to know that her heart and soul belonged to him, surely, he would use it to break her further than she could possibly have been broken before.

Raising her hands to his chest, she pushed him away with all her might. After a moment, he stepped towards her again, uttering her name. In response she stepped back and held her hands up to halt him.

"Connie please."

"I think it would be best if we did not speak of the matter any longer, we clearly will not be in agreement as to our opinions on it."

Connie saw the panic in his eyes as he realised his manipulations were coming to an end. Deciding to pre-empt any further betrayals, Connie sought to begin a new stage for their marriage.

"I feel we have been too wrapped up in ourselves and so have been residing in a fantasy world." Confusion crossed his features. "I do not know of any marriage in society where the husband lies in his wife's bed every night. I think, therefore, that we should reside in separate rooms."

Connie's heart broke at every word she spoke. "I shall not deny you your husbandly rights, I simply ask that when you have…. finished your business…that you return to your own rooms."

Sensing that her resolve was about to break, Connie quickly sped past her husband to return to the house.

She ignored him as he attempted to call her back and darted through the house to her rooms, locking her bedroom door behind her.

Connie collapsed onto the bed and prepared for the onslaught of tears. They stilled, however, as she heard the rattle of the doorknob.

For what seemed to be an eternity, Connie stared at the door, sensing him stood on the other side, waiting for her to let him in. Hearing footsteps that grew fainter, Connie realised that he had given up and she allowed the tears to wash over her.

Xander locked himself in his library for the rest of the day, commiserating in how dreadful everything had gone.

The worst thing was that he knew there was very little he could do about it. Connie had seen him being kissed and molested by another woman. He could not rely on said woman to tell his wife the entire thing was one-sided and so all he could do was tell Connie that he did not reciprocate Lady Walker's advances and hope she believed him.

It appeared that she did not.

He resolved that even if it took twenty years for his wife to trust him again, Xander would wait faithfully. And in the meantime, he would indulge in all the alcohol at his disposal.

He did not know how many hours had passed but at some point, Xander had looked to the window to see that moonlight spilled into the room rather than the sunbeams he expected.

In his drunken stupor, all Xander could think about was that this was the one time of day that Connie had said she would allow him entry. Therefore, he began his staggered walk across the house to his wife's rooms.

Knocking on the door, Xander leant against it waiting for his wife to grant him entry. As a result of this, when Connie opened the door, he fell forwards and somehow managed to manoeuvre the pair to fall onto the bed instead of the floor.

Propping himself on one arm over her, he spoke. "I have come to claim my rights!"

Anger crossed Connie's face as she shoved him back and moved to stand. "Don't you dare come near me!" Xander chuckled at how she appeared to struggle not to shout. Nothing would horrify his wife more than risking the servants gossiping about them.

Lifting himself so he sat facing her, Xander lifted his eyebrows in a challenge. "Did you or did you not say I could come here to claim my husbandly rights?"

"I am not allowing a drunkard into my bed." She shrieked.

Getting to his feet, Xander stalked towards her. "Sobriety was not one of your terms, wife. Now come here." With that Xander took Connie into his arms, ignoring her attempts to break free.

"Let go of me right now." "No." "The only way you will have me tonight is by force, do you honestly wish that to occur?"

He paused at her words and loosened his grip, although not enough to release her. "Connie," he beckoned, "let me make love to you." A flicker of emotion flashed in her eyes at his words, and he searched her gaze as he waited for her response.

"Please do not make me do this." Her eyes flickered shut as a tear fell down her cheek. Xander leant forward to place a light kiss where it fell.

"Then kiss me," he responded, "and let it be a real kiss. Imagine you are kissing me before this wretched day happened."

As soon as the words left his lips, Connie's mouth pressed onto his and her tongue clashed violently with his. He groaned as their bodies melded together and her hands lifted to run through his hair.

Xander could not say what exactly it was, but they shared a mutual sense of need to possess one another. Raw hunger overtook them as lips, tongues and teeth clashed in a need for more. Xander jolted as he then felt her small hand grasp his manhood and begin frantically rubbing him through his trousers.

Wrenching his mouth away from hers, he buried his head in her neck as she began to lick and nibble at his ear.

"Do you know what it feels like?" She breathlessly said. "Since the first moment you laid your hands on me, every inch of me has been possessed by you. No other man has ever touched me. All my body knows is how to pleasure you and only you!"

Xander began thrusting into her hand and he listened to her words, feeling a sense of triumph at how she was his.

"I wish I knew how it felt, to be the only person in your lover's entire universe." He began to suck on her neck, feeling a sudden urge to mark her as his. "Oh god, it drives me mad with jealousy that you've known other women. Seeing her with you today reminded me of that."

His head rose ever so slightly to answer her, "Feel how hard I am, Connie. No one else gets me like this." He lifted his head further to kiss her. "No one makes me come as hard as you do." Their movements at his crotch descended into sporadic chaos. "Your lips are so plump that I could not bear to kiss another woman. Your breasts are the perfect size for my hands to hold. And, dear god, you have the tightest quim I have ever come across."

Xander's words were drawn to a temporary halt as he spent himself in his trousers and her hand gradually slowed its movements to draw his pleasure out even longer.

When he caught his breath, Xander grasped Connie's hair to pull her head back to look up at him. He gave her the most intense stare as he finished. "I have known women before you, Constance, but no man in his right mind could have you and then move on to another woman. Every inch of you consumes me!"

Her cheeks reddened and desire pooled in her eyes as she took in his words. He lowered his hands as she pushed him to release her and turned to face away from him.

"You've had your kiss," came her husky reply, "now leave me."

Xander cleared his throat and turned to leave. As his hand touched the doorknob, she spoke again.

"Unless we have a social engagement, do not presume to seek my company outside of this room."

His jaw clenched in anger.

"I believe there is an exhibit in three days, see that you behave yourself."

Xander was angry over the change in circumstances, now he was furious at her callous words.

"The Duchess of Bristol expects us for dinner the day after tomorrow, see that you behave yourself then."

Connie finally turned back to him as she understood his words. He could see her nostrils flaring in anger and she began to breathe heavily.

Her words were strained as she spoke, seeming to attempt to quell exactly how angry she was. "I will never dine with that family!"

His jaw dropped at the nerve of her. "I am your husband and if I say you are to dine with the Ainsworth's you will do so and gladly!"

"So, you will not allow me to refuse?" Her eyes met his in a challenge.

"No."

"Very well, I shall arrange for my belongings to be moved to my parent's home and shall resume living with them."

The anger was growing greater and greater and Xander saw that if he did not remove himself from the room soon, he would do something he would deeply regret.

Sensing that this was a battle he would not win, he decided to give into his wife on this occasion...under one condition.

"Very well, I shall give Verity your apologies for not being able to attend." He then opened the door and stepped outside before delivering his parting words. "I expect in the morning that when I wake, it will be to find you in my bed with that pretty little mouth wrapped around my cock. I might as well get something out of this marriage!"

Before she could say anything further, he slammed the door behind him and stalked to his rooms.

If Connie was determined that the only way that she would be his wife was in the bedroom, then he was damn well going to make sure he took her so often that she would struggle to walk!

Chapter Nineteen

A new routine had formed in Chalmers House to reflect the state of the couple's marriage. Gone were the jovial talks and playful flirting, in its place was stilted silence and a sense of misery reeking through the house.

The sudden embraces and lovemaking remained, however. Connie bitterly thought of how the actions remained, but the motives changed. Her husband now pulled her into his embraces to exercise his rights, for he could have her no other way. And Connie herself welcomed him, for it was now the only way she could share affection with the man she loved.

Her pride suffered, of course, knowing he was essentially using her body, but she craved the passion they shared and the few moments, after the act, when they could be loving and affectionate with one another, sharing in the afterglow of their lovemaking.

Connie did all she could to distract herself from her estrangement. Every time Rachel asked for her help in her mother's ventures she would leap at the chance. She accepted every invitation sent to her and, on rare free evenings, she chose to visit with family rather than dine alone.

Whilst it largely distracted her from her troubles, there was once person that revelled in constantly reminding her of her misery: The Dowager Countess.

The woman had begun to emerge from her rooms once the renovations had been completed, as she had hosted several afternoon teas with her lady friends where she had irritatingly taken all credit for Connie's hard work.

Of course, the woman had become positively gleeful once she had realised that the newlyweds were no longer blissfully happy with one another. As much as Connie tried to avoid the woman she could not always succeed. Worse was the fact that they would most likely come across one another in company and so the Dowager Countess revelled in making some snide remark to humiliate her.

The most recent insult came at a ball held by Baroness Bertram, an event considered by most to be the highlight of the season. Connie had attempted the sneak past her mother-in-law as she held court with her clan of worshippers. Unfortunately, the woman spotted her and beckoned her forward. She had started with platitudes, playing the doting mother-in-law but no-one could deny the true meaning when she gushed over how wonderful Connie was at "not culling her husband's social endeavours" by allowing him to "continue on his nightly jaunts with his friends."

For the rest of the night Connie had felt as though she were being constantly watched and she was sure she was the current target of gossip. A belief that was confirmed the following morning when she met Jane for brunch.

"If I can offer you any advice," Jane had said, "it is to pay no notice of what people are saying. I spent the first year of my marriage practically in tears over what was said and now I refuse to indulge it. I am far happier as a result."

Connie did not have the heart to tell her that the gossip of Jane's marriage most likely was seen as evidence for the gossip regarding hers. She counted herself lucky that Harry was off fighting in the continent and Duncan had no intentions of ever marrying. Lest the gossip affect their prospects.

Feeling more hopeless by the day, Connie decided the seek the advice of her mother, who had wisely decided to stand back and wait for Connie to approach her rather than provide unsolicited advice.

Arriving at her childhood home, Jennings advised Connie that her mother was in the garden. Connie found her mother in the process of painting a watercolour and admired how well her mother had conveyed the beauty of the roses.

"If you do not wish to keep the painting, Mama, then I shall be glad to take it." She leant down to kiss her mother's cheek before taking a seat.

"I should like that very much, my sweet," Cora smiled warmly at her, "it would perhaps look lovely in a nursery, do you think?"

Connie laughed, "Oh yes, my child will be able to have my favourite part of home with them every day."

"Favourite part of home?" Cora admonished, "So I come after your great-grandmother's rose bush then I take it?"

"Of course, it was my refuge whenever I was in trouble."

"Well, I am sure your little one will find their own refuge in the famous Chalmers gardens, will they not?"

"If they are anything like I was," the thought troubled Connie, "I am not sure I would like my child to be like me though."

Cora turned in her seat to fully face her daughter and reached over to take her hand. "My daughter is beautiful, intelligent, graceful, kind and everything I ever wished for. I could not be more proud of you, my sweet. I am sure you would be blessed to have a daughter like yourself."

"A daughter who gives herself to complete strangers at balls, risking her family's ruin. Is it that sort of daughter you mean, Mama?" Connie lamented. "Or perhaps it is the kind of daughter whose actions lead to the breaking of a perfectly good engagement? Or the kind who cannot keep her husband interested in her after only a month of marriage? And cannot fathom how to approach him for any sort of help with her troubles? And finds herself the centre of gossip in all of society? Should I wish for that sort of a daughter Mama?" Connie did not realise she had not stopped to take a breath until she finished.

Seeing her mother's worried eyes gazing upon her, Connie felt tears begin to rise and she barely managed to speak before they burst out. "Mama, what am I to do?"

Standing up, Cora wrapped her arms around her weeping daughter and rubbed her back soothingly as she waited for the tears to cease.

After several minutes, Connie found she could cry no more and looked up as her mother reached down to wipe away her tears.

Kneeling before her daughter, Cora took her hands before speaking. "Now, miss Constance, what are we to do with you?"

"I was rather hoping you would tell me." Connie admitted.

"Sweetheart, there are two people in this world who can help you solve your problems, and I am not one of them."

"Well, you're no use are you Mama?" Connie sniffled, eliciting a soft laugh from the older woman.

"You know, when I married your father, my mother gave me one piece of advice." Cora tucked her daughter's hair behind her ear as she spoke. "She said that I should endeavour never to go to bed angry with my husband."

"Oh," Connie considered the advice, seeing its merits, "well that is quite….."

"Useless? Oh, I agree." He mother balked, "Do you know how many times I went to bed absolutely furious at something your father had done and then woken up in the morning feeling less inclined to yell and more inclined to talk? Far more times than I care to admit to."

"So, you suggest that next time I am angry with Xander that I wait until the morning to speak with him?"

"No, what I am saying is that you should not seek my advice on any matters regarding your husband." Connie grew more confused. "Because the Earl is not your father, and I am not you. We are not the same people therefore we will solve any problems in different ways."

Connie grew despondent hearing her mother would not help. "So, I am to live in misery then? Not knowing how my husband will be one day from the next?"

"Connie, dearest, you and your husband did not start your marriage happy, but happiness grew. Perhaps you should think back to how that happened?"

Cora moved back to her seat as Connie mused aloud. "We were both afraid that we were detested by each other over being forced into the marriage. I recall realising that he did not abhor me when he revealed how much he wan…....."

215

Connie had to stop herself before revealing delicate matters to her mother.

"What did he reveal, my sweet?" Cora pursed her lips with a knowing glint in her eye.

"That we shared an attraction." Connie cringed that she was discussing this with her mother. "And then the attraction developed into affection I suppose."

"Well, there you have it, find some commonality you share and use it open up to one another. How simple."

Not as simple as her mother might believe, Connie rued. Making love was what allowed her and Xander to bond initially but they were still making love now. It clearly was not developing into anything further than a more insatiable bond of lust.

"Have you begun your plans for the child yet? That could help."

Connie cringed even further, "No, I have not actually told him yet, I am afraid."

"Oh, how wonderful." Cora clapped her hands together in joy, her green eyes glistening. "You can go tell your husband you are to be parents; he will hug and kiss you in celebration and you can use it to begin life afresh."

"I am not too sure a child will solve our problems, Mama." Connie suddenly found herself jolted out of her chair as her mother escorted her through the house blabbering about how wonderful a bond children give their parents, not giving Connie any chance to speak.

Before Connie knew it, she was ushered into her carriage on her way home to tell her husband the good news, to which she felt a bout of nausea begin to take hold.

Upon her arrival, Connie meandered to her husband's office, supposing that if he were in at all he would be there.

To her surprise, she peered in the open doorway to see him sat at his desk, furiously scribbling away. She took the opportunity to observe him whilst he remained unaware of her presence.

His torso was covered only by a white shirt, the top few buttons were undone showing a hint of his chest hair and his sleeves were rolled up, allowing Connie to see the tight muscles of his arms. Connie bit her lip as a wave of lust came over her at the sight of him.

His attention was unwavering in whatever it was he was writing. His brow was furrowed and his shoulders tense in his focus. Connie decided that she would solve three problems in one: their marriage woes, her sudden lust, and his stresses.

She swayed into the room and his eyes briefly flicked up in surprise that she should seek him out.

"Whatever it is, Connie, would you mind waiting? I need to go over these accounts to see what spare funds we have after the renovations." Connie was perturbed that he did not once look at her as he spoke.

Unwavering in her goal, she moved around the desk to stand behind him as she responded in an attempt of sultriness, "Is there anything I can help you with?" She began to rub his shoulders. "I believe I know of a rather enjoyable way to relief you of tension."

Xander dropped his quill as his head twisted to look up at her suspiciously. "Why are you being nice to me?"

"I have been going through a bout a cravings recently," she bent over to run her fingers over his exposed chest, "yesterday I had a distinct hankering for apples, this morning I thought I would die if I did not get any biscuits. Right now, however, I find myself in a desperate need for something only my husband can give me."

She looked down to see his throat move as he gulped. "W…why should that be, do you suppose?" He seemed to struggle to speak as he relaxed into her ministrations.

"I was unsure at first, but my Mama assures me that such cravings are quite common when one is expecting a child."

"Oh, is that so?" Xander breathlessly asked, clearly not taking in her words. It took several moments of waiting before Connie could feel him tense under her hands and he comprehended her meaning.

He jumped out of his seat in a flash and turned to face her. "Connie......are you jesting?" She shook her head, beaming with joy. "We're having a child?"

She could barely voice her confirmation before she was wrapped in his arms and twirled in the air. She was then promptly placed back on the ground as her husband began panicking that he may have hurt her, to which she had to reassure him that she was well.

Looking into one another's eyes, Connie felt a rush of emotion swarm over her as she felt the bond between them being strengthened. For the first time in several weeks, she knew everything would be fine.

Xander rubbed his hands up and down her arms as he spoke. "Is this really happening? We are going to have a child?"

"Yes, darling." Connie was closed to tears. "Believe it or not you are going to be father." Xander froze as he processed her words. She began to worry as his face paled and he released her to lean against the desk.

"Dear god, I am going to be a father. I do not know how to be a father. Oh lord, how can I have a child, I am still a child myself! Connie, what are we going to do, we cannot do this!" Connie let him ramble and she reached over the desk to fetch his drink.

After ensuring he drank every last drop of brandy, Connie took his face in her hands and reassured him. "You are going to be an excellent father and we are going to love and provide for our child, and all will be well."

Xander dopily smiled at her as he moved his hands atop hers and whispered, "I think you're wonderful, you know."

If Connie's heart had not melted before, it was in a puddle now. Rising to plant a soft kiss upon his lips, she then pushed him back onto the chair and sat on his lap, smoothing her skirts over and he stared at her stomach.

Crooking her finger under his chin, Connie titled it up to greet his lips in a prolonged kiss. When they finally parted, Connie found herself staring into his eyes and realised that there was nothing she wished to do more than tell him how much she was in love with him.

Xander, however, began musing aloud plans for the child, disrupting her intentions. Resting her head on his shoulder, she smiled to herself as she imagined their future with all the plans her husband was describing.

If the child were a boy, he would be named after her father, attend Charterhouse like Xander did, he would have all the finest horses and the best tutors' money could pay for.

A girl on the other hand, Xander said, would be dressed in the finest silks and satins imported from all over the world. She would have her own personal dancing teacher and an entire room just for her dolls.

No matter what the child was they would want for nothing. Their birthdays would be the grandest of affairs, the envy of all indeed. With their mother's beauty *(Connie had to roll her eyes)* and their father's wealth, no doubt they would be the greatest catch when they chose to wed.

Connie was thrilled when Xander announced that Jane would be the godmother, but it then felt as though a cold bucket of water was poured onto her as he decided the godfather would be Liam Ainsworth.

Connie realised that if she did not put her foot down now, her children would end up in the throes of the devil himself.

Lifting herself up on his lap, Connie brought her husband out of his musings. "Darling, I need you to promise me something. It's awfully important."

"Anything you wish, flower." Xander answered, smiling up at her.

"Promise me you will never let any of the Ainsworths near our child." Connie knew she had to look him in the eyes as she spoke, but she wished she did not. All hopes and dreams she had for their future came crashing down alongside his features as he took in what she was saying.

Xander gently moved her off his lap and stood before her. "You know I cannot do that, Constance."

"You said you would always choose me." Panic rose in her voice. "You know that as long as you allow those people in our lives that you are not choosing me. We are never going to be happy as long as they are lurking in the background!"

"Connie, if I choose you now, I'll only end up hating you in the end." Connie's heart broke at hearing the defeat in his voice. "You are asking me to choose between you and the people I consider my family, who love me unconditionally. I'm sorry, petal, but you will never win."

"Please, Xander, think about the family you are putting aside. What about us?" Connie grabbed his hand to rest it against her stomach.

"I would kill for you and our little one, but I will not be unhappy. I know what it is like to be a child of unhappy, resentful parents and I will not do that to my own child."

Connie moved away from him, tears forming as she spoke. "Instead, you will force your child to suffer through your choice then?"

"No Connie, if we are being honest, it is your choice that will make us suffer." With those words, Xander took her arm and walked her out the door before closing it between the two, leaving his wife feeling more hopeless than ever.

Chapter Twenty

The day Xander and his wife came to the sad realisation that they would not be able to reconcile with each other's views regarding the Ainsworth family, he spent hours pouring himself into his accounts.

The next day he went to his club, where he spent several hours drinking and gambling. The following day he remained abed nursing the worst hangover of his life. As he lay in bed, Xander decided that the worst thing he could do for his child was to be a drunk.

Therefore, when he awoke the next morning, he rose, broke his fast alone and then left the house to go for a ride. Once he returned home, he changed and went to his office to go over any investment figures or household accounts that needed his attention. In the afternoon, he partook in several bouts of fencing, followed by dinner with his adoptive family.

All his subsequent days were filled with the same routine. There would be an occasional variance, perhaps instead of fencing he chose to box, or he needed to go to a meeting regarding his investments, but by and large the routine remained the same. As July neared to a close, more changes occurred. The 1809 season came to an end and so preparations begun for the household to return to his seat in Bedfordshire.

Xander rarely saw his wife. He had soon realised that even if he limited their encounters to carnal relations, his heart would continue to break at how distant they had become and so, aside from the few social occasions attended together and brief encounters in passing, they did not interact with one another.

The doctor had visited thrice. Each time he had been informed of the visit beforehand by his valet and so he endeavoured to be at home on each occasion, where he would discuss any developments or needs with the man once he had finished seeing Connie.

The season came to a close with a ball hosted by the Ainsworths. Connie outright refused to attend and so Xander had used her pregnancy as an excuse when anyone enquired after her, although he was sure his mother was gleefully gossiping once his back was turned.

As he entered the house on the humid Wednesday evening, his mother on his arm, Xander marvelled at how Verity had outdone herself this year. The invitation had specified that all the women should wear white, and the men wear black. The theme became clear as he observed all the servers dressed as various chess pieces, he saw several rooks, knights and bishops dotted around.

He passed several spectacles on his way to the garden, where a chessboard dance floor had been constructed. There was a bishop contortionist fitting her body through an unstrung racket, a chorus of opera singing rooks and the entrance to the garden was outlined by a pair of fire-breathing knights.

Spotting Baron Philpott engaged in what appeared to be a heated debate with Sir Edward Branson, Xander headed over to rescue Colette's husband.

He gave Larry a pair of hard pats on the back as he interrupted the pair. "Philpott, my man, I hope you have not left your wife and son all alone in Kent tonight?"

Relief etched onto Larry's face at the disruption. "I wouldn't dream of it," he replied. "Colette informed me that we were returning because she would not miss her mother's ball."

"Oh good, I was considering taking a detour to Bloomfield's when we would return home to see all was well but now, I do not need to!"

"Is a diversion to Kent when on your way to Bedfordshire not drastically out of your way? And were you planning of informing us ahead of time of your visit?" His tone was reprimanding but Xander thought the beam on his friend's face was more indicative of his true feelings.

"I'm sure any problems you would have would be immediately waived at the happiness on your wife's face."

"Hmmm." Larry's eyes narrowed and lips pursed in mock distaste.

"Well, it matters not now, in any case." Xander declared. "I can annoy you with questions on fatherhood now, instead."

"Ah, I did hear. Congratulations Sutton." Xander shook the outstretched hand. "When is the newest terror expected to enter the world then?"

"Oh, around February-March time I believe." *Or a month earlier.* "If it's a girl, shall we arrange a betrothal now and avoid the headaches later?"

Larry chuckled at the prospect. "You're forgetting that I could negotiate a hefty dowry, I could bribe Calvert for your investment details."

"Slight problem with that plan, chum, you can't bribe a man who already can get everything he wants!"

"No quite everythi......" Larry paused as his head turned left, bemusement crossed his face. "Where the devil did Branson go?" The pair searched the room for the man. Deciding that he could not be found, Xander shrugged with a comment of "No one's complaining."

"Where is your wife anyway?" Larry queried, collected a pair of champagne glasses from a passing bishop and handing one to Xander.

He took a sip before answering, "Officially, she is abed due to her condition." "And unofficially?" "She has allowed her irrational hatred of your in-laws to render her a hermit in a ruined marriage."

Not wishing to discuss his wife any further, Xander spoke before Larry could respond. "Speaking of your in-law's, where might they be lurking?"

"The king and queen? Off holding court, I imagine." Larry smirked.

"Don't let the gossipers hear you say that, we don't want to bring on another bout for His Majesty now do we?"

"You haven't worked it out yet then, I assume?" Xander titled his head in confusion, prompting further explanation. "There are six pieces in chess: king, queen, knight, bishop, rook and pawn. Now, the servants are dressed up as knights, rooks, and bishops. So that leaves our beloved hosts as the king and queen, and we are all pawns in their game."

Xander chortled as the idea. "Even the Duke and Duchess are not *that* delusional!"

"Delusional? No." Larry said. "Verity just likes the idea of being queen for the night. My father-in-law, on the other hand, I think it rather feeds his ego to be considered the king, ruling all beneath him."

"Now that is the most accurate description of my father, I do believe I've ever heard." Both men jumped at the sudden appearance of Lady Eliza Ainsworth, who was casually resting a champagne glass against her lips, and she observed the pair.

"Does your mother know you're drifting from the lemonade, sister?" Larry admonished, taking her glass, and pouring the contents into his own.

The woman waved her hand in dismissal, "Oh, it does not matter. If I get too inebriated, I shall simply be discreetly escorted to my room."

"I do not think you can be discreet wearing that dress, Eliza." Xander said, "You do know that the invitation explicitly said to wear white?"

Indeed, Eliza had chosen to wear a dress of deep green, ensuring that all eyes would naturally be drawn to her.

"Yes, however, I did recently discover that I have a distant ancestor hailing from Ireland and thought to reflect my newfound heritage."

Her eyes darted back and forth between the two men and once she realised that they were not even going to pretend to entertain her excuse, she pouted and declared that they were "no fun at all!"

"Mama thought it would profit my marriage prospects if I dressed to draw the attention of all the eligible men here tonight."

"She wishes for you to catch a man's eye?" She nodded to Xander's question. "At the very last event of the season before everyone returns to their country homes?"

"I thought it ridiculous too, but she thinks several months of solely written correspondence would prolong interest."

"Otherwise known as love letters?" Larry mused, "Don't young ladies find that romantic?" Eliza balked at his suggestion.

"Not this young lady!"

"You know what I think, Sutton. I believe Verity is punishing her impertinent daughter for her flirtations with the Wexford boy this season." Larry smirked as Eliza's eyes briefly widened before returning to feigning disinterest.

"Harry? Good lord, he left London two months ago."

"And I have been despondent ever since." Eliza sighed wistfully. "How is his sister, in any case?" Xander cringed at the new topic of conversation.

"Have you not heard, sister dear? She refuses to venture into Ainsworth territory as she believes you would lure her into the kitchen to be cooked and eaten."

Eliza's nose wrinkled at the prospect, "Wexford's would require a fair amount of seasoning I imagine." Both men boomed with laughter at the thought.

"Does she really believe we are that horrid though? I did not think I had that much power over people." Eliza pondered, "I know that I can make some barbarous remarks, but I always believed people thought me irritating rather than frightening."

"Shame you couldn't have used some of that charm to quiz Harry as to his family's views." Xander was then struck by the hurt that appeared to cross his companion's face. "Surely you are not going to let my wife's silly ideas upset you?"

"No, it is just that," Eliza hesitated, "I had thought that my helping in your…...troubles……at first would have prompted her to perhaps reconsider her perceptions, at least where I was concerned. It appears I was wrong."

"There must be something deeper at play here," Larry decided, "people do not develop these irrational fears out of nowhere, there must be something going on that the rest of us have no knowledge of."

Xander considered his friend's words. Connie had never explained exactly what her reasoning was regarding the Ainsworth family. In fact, she simply tended to panic whenever the topic was broached. He did not dare allow a hope for reconciliation emerge, but a small flicker began for at least some understanding.

"Well, I do not care what she has been taught!" Eliza announced, "I will bother her until she likes me." Xander pinched the bridge of his nose in a bid to quell the laughter bumbling up. He thought that Eliza may be getting her hopes up slightly too high in this regard.

Clearly, Larry had felt the same, as his response was to pinch her cheek and tease. "You cannot stamp your foot and scream your way into someone's affections, little one."

A scathing look was directed his way in response which then turned to focus on Xander. Darting her eyes back and forth between the two men, Eliza muttered under her breath, "You'll see......You'll all see...." And she promptly slinked off, presumably to go scheme with her cousin, whom Xander believed had much more of a chance of winning his wife over.

Turning back to one another, eyes dancing with amusement, the two men chortled at the departing woman.

"Perhaps you should get down to the source of the problem then." Xander drained the rest of his glass as he considered Larry's suggestion.

"I anticipate that discussion with glee, 'Good day, Wexford, tell me why do you have an irrational hatred of people I love and admire?'"

"You love and admire me? I am touched." Larry placed his hand over his heart in mock delight.

"Only you, my darling Baron." Xander teased.

"Food for thought, though." Larry's head tilted as something in the distance caught his eye. "Excuse me, chap, it appears my father-in-law has decided to disturb my son's sleep to show him off."

Xander did not get an opportunity to utter his goodbyes as Larry rushed over to rescue his screaming child.

Grabbing another glass of champagne, he ventured to a corner of the garden and leant against a Grecian statue to take a minute to consider his prospects.

If he did not resolve the disagreement as soon as possible, Xander risked his child being tugged back and forth between parents who would continue to whisper opposing opinions in their ear.

If Connie could not have her mind changed, then he risked having his only child estranged from him, Xander could not bear to consider the prospect.

Chapter Twenty-One

Connie had come decided that the carriage ride to Xander's country seat was perhaps the most excruciating of her life.

She spent almost the entire day struggling to prevent herself from emptying the contents of her stomach, a feat not helped by the bumps in the road. If this were not insufferable enough, she also had to deal with being the only company for the Dowager Countess and so was forced to endure the veiled insults the woman spewed at her.

If she chose to direct her gaze to the carriage window, her view was marred by the sight of her husband, who was riding on horseback alongside the carriage.

She found herself glancing his way on several occasions, longing to be able to hold him and return to the affections they held at the beginning of their marriage. For one moment, Connie's thoughts had drifted to happier times, and she was horrified to discover her husband's eyes meeting hers. Her cheeks reddened as she wondered exactly how long she had been staring and for how long he had noticed.

As the carriage drew to the front steps of the house, Connie was relieved and looked forward to relaxing in a long, hot bath and then sleeping until noon the next day.

She inwardly groaned, however, the second she stepped out of the carriage and found the servants lined up, prepared to be introduced to their new mistress. Seeing Mrs Potter at the head of the line, she knew she would not be able to escape having the house tour immediately.

Resigned to her fate, she plastered a smile on her face, attempted to smooth any wrinkles on her grey travelling dress and resolved to make the tour as quick and painless as humanly possible.

She grew more thankful throughout the tour that the décor was in complete contrast to the one that greeted her when she first arrived at Chalmer's House. There was not a single eyesore in sight, and she was positive that none of the rooms would be giving her husband a headache.

Upon further enquiry, it appeared her mother-in-law had made a habit of spending only two weeks at the house. Once that period had concluded, she would begin visiting her lady friends before returning to London for the yuletide season. As a result, she had not felt the need to inflict her unique taste on the household.

It was queer, then, that the Dowager Countess had announced in the carriage that she planned to spend several months in residence. Connie had the distinct impression that she was one of the reasons for the change in plans.

Excusing herself with a headache, Connie retreated to her rooms before she could be led into the gardens. Relieved to be able to finally rest, she twisted the doorknob to enter her domain.

Looking around, Connie found herself in a grand room, decorated in pale blue and white colours. The large four-poster bed appeared warm and inviting and Connie's feet moved of their own accord over in preparation of collapsing onto the accommodating sheets and pillows. She enveloped herself into the softness of the bed and felt herself drifting off to sleep.

Connie was wakened from her dreamless state by a hand on her shoulder, jolted her back and forth. She blinked several times as her eyes adjusted to the darkness that eclipsed the room, the only hint of light being the moonlight streaking through the windows.

Coming to, she found herself staring up at the brutal eyes of her mother-in-law.

"What, in god's name, do you think you are doing in my bed?" Connie winced as the voice appeared to reach pitches previously unknown to man.

Connie stifled a yawn as she answered, "Your bed? I do not understand." The sheets were harshly whipped off her body and hands gripped her arm as she was dragged from the bed.

Taking a moment to find her footing once she was released, Connie swept her hair from her face. "What on earth is wrong with you?"

"What is wrong with you?" Came the bitter response, "The Earl and I waited over an hour for you to show your face for dinner. Our food was cold by the time we gave up and ate without you. And now I find that you neglected us so you could defile my bed instead of your own!"

"Your bed? I was told these were the rooms of the countess."

"Yes, they are, hence why they are my rooms and THAT is my bed." Connie had enough of the woman.

"YOU ARE NOT THE COUNTESS; I AM AND I AM GOING TO TAKE THE ROOMS AS IS MY RIGHT!" Her mother-in-law took a step back, wide-eyed at her outburst.

Connie was taken aback herself; she did not think she had yelled at anyone since she was in leading strings and partial to tantrums. She took a moment to gather a sense of calm before continuing the disagreement.

"I apologise if it causes you any annoyances, but the fact remains that these are the rooms designated for the Countess of Sutton and as the current holder of that title, I am the one who should reside here."

"These are my rooms and I refu……"

"I do not care if you refuse to accept that these are my rooms now or that you are clearly threatened by the fact that you have been replaced in almost every sense in this household. The sooner you come to terms with the fact that you no longer have unopposed power, the better for the both of us!"

A chill crept down her spine as the elder woman's eyes narrowed and her icy glare tore into Connie's sense of calm. Her words were cool and cutting.

"I do not care that you are the daughter of a duke. I do not care that you are young and beautiful. Your reputation for kindness and charity matters naught with me." The Dowager Countess' nose practically touched Connie's own as she invaded her personal space. "Everything you have touched in this family has turned to dust. Have you not wondered why my other sons never visit? Why they stay away from *your* household?"

Connie did not want to hear the answer. "They have seen their brother forced into an unwanted marriage with a wife who behaves so coldly to him that he cannot bear to spend any waking moment in his own home. They hear gossip every day regarding his misery and so they stay away lest they be infected by your poison too."

"Leave these rooms now!" Connie urged.

The older woman leaned in to whisper in Connie's ear. "I hope that bastard you're carrying dies. I hope it comes out so deformed that no one will be able to deny that it is the child of a she-devil."

Smack

The sound of the slap Connie gave her mother-in-law pierced the room. She followed it by dragging the woman by the arm to the open doorway and pushing her out of the door so hard that the older woman fell onto her backside.

As much as Connie would have liked to see the expression on the woman's face, she instead chose to slam and lock the door to prevent any further escalations.

Attempting to return to the bed, Connie collapsed halfway there into a foetal position and spent several moments alternating between sobs and struggles to regain her breath.

Panic coursed through her veins for her unborn child as she realised that, if the Dowager Countess were not making idle threats, she would need to leave the house as soon as possible lest she risk life and limb.

Connie did not sleep for the remainder of the night. She remained in the same position on the floor until the faint sounds of birds began to rise and the dawn light crept into the room.

Rising to open the door of her dressing room, Connie was dismayed to find that the clothes it kept were those of the Dowager Countess and not her own.

Forgoing the temptation to find a change of clothes, Connie walked back to unlock the entrance to the rooms and cautiously peered outside to see if any dangers lay in wait for her.

Sensing she was safe, Connie crept along the hallway and down the stairs to let herself out of the house. Breathing in the fresh country air, she rounded the house, lamenting that she had not thought to put on her shoes before leaving her temporary sanctuary.

Reaching the stables, Connie called out to attract the attention of the stable master, who was hurriedly putting on his shirt as he rushed out to greet her.

"Good day, Your Grace. My apologies, I did not know you would wish to take an early morning ride."

The man's eyes drifted up and down her person as he took in her rumpled clothes, unruly hair, bare feet, and no doubt sleep-deprived eyes. Connie could only imagine how much of a sight she appeared to him.

"There is no need for apologies." She resisted the urge to smooth her clothes and hair. "I have decided to visit my family's estate as soon as possible and request that you ready the carriage to leave immediately."

Eyebrows rose and his jolted back head in surprise. "Are your family's estates not in Gloucestershire, Ma'am? I do not think we should be ready to journey that far without a large amount of preparation."

Panic set in at his words. Connie needed to leave Bedfordshire as soon as possible!

"If the horses are not ready for a long journey, then we will travel until we reach a stable where horses who are ready can be purchased."

"Very well, Ma'am." The man replied. "Once you have returned after dressing for travel, we will be ready to leave."

"I am dressed for travel now!" Connie's voice rose. "I am giving you and your men ten minutes to be ready. Whomever is ready first will find his wages tripled with effect immediately."

Giving a firm nod of assent, the man sped away shouting orders, bringing the peaceful stables into chaos.

Connie felt bad for her rudeness and made a mental note to raise his earnings as well......and learn his name! Perching on a near stool, Connie bit her nails and tried to distract her thoughts from her grumbling stomach. She would not feel safe until she was far away from the lands.

A record six minutes later, Connie was being assisted into the freshly prepared carriage. Connie was touched to find extra cushions and blankets resting on the seats to make her more comfortable. Settling into the seats, she turned to the open carriage door to find a footman leaning into the carriage, holding out a basket to her.

Taking the basket, she lifted the cloth covering it to find an array of sandwiches and fruits prepared for her.

Turning back to the man, tears filling her eyes, Connie's voice shook as she gave him her thanks.

Seeing pity in the eyes looking back at her, Connie wondered what the servants must be thinking about her. As the carriage began to move, she imagined that they must be either horrified or embarrassed at how their new mistress appeared to be nothing but a frightened child, running home to her parents.

Xander knew something was wrong as soon as he stepped into the breakfast room. Servants were sharing meaningful looks when they thought he was not looking and, worst of all, his mother was sat at the table waiting for him.

Taking his time filling up his plate, he decided that he would not give in to whatever schemes his mother had in her head this week and ignore her until she said what she had clearly disrupted her morning routine to say.

Taking his seat, Xander tucked into his food as he beckoned the butler over to his side.

"Tell me McCawley, have you found all in order in the estate?"

"Yes, Your Grace." Xander's brow furrowed at how rushed the man's answer was. His mother began buttering her toast as loud as possible in an effort to gain his attention.

"And have the servants settled into their rooms well?" The butler answered in the affirmative.

"I assume the countess is breaking her fast in her rooms?" Xander enquired, hoping his tone was casual as he asked after his wife. He had decided before they left London that he would dedicate the day to resolving their marriage woes and knew she would be in better spirits if her stomach was full.

"The countess left for her parents' estate this morning, My Lord."

Xander's hand froze on its way to his mouth and his fork dropped back to the plate with a clatter.

"I'm sorry I do not believe I heard you correctly, McCawley. For some strange reason I thought you said that my wife had left." Xander chuckled disbelievingly. The laugh soon left his lips as he looked up and observed his butler looking sheepishly at him, confirming that he had heard correctly.

Xander was gobsmacked. He leant back in his seat as he processed what this meant: His wife had left him!

Naturally, he was not allowed to fully process his thoughts as his mother finally decided to speak up.

"I imagine she is running away in fear rather than facing up to the consequences of her actions." Xander's eyes drifted to see her smirking as she sipped on her tea.

"What actions, mother?"

"She attacked me in the middle of the night," his mother clearly feigned distress as she spoke, "she struck me, and I found myself lying on the floor in pain from a second attack. It was most upsetting." She wiped away fake tears.

"What did you do to deserve the treatment?"

"There is nothing I could have done to prompt such a vicious attack. I am the victim in this instance!"

Xander crossed his arms as he stared straight at the woman sat before him. Without taking his eyes off her, he spoke to McCawley. "Have a carriage prepared to travel to Gloucestershire and arrange for my mother's belongings to be packed and readied for her to return to London."

His mother looked incredulous as the butler left the room to carry out his orders.

"You are not turning me out of my own home!"

"When we are in Bedfordshire, your home is in the dower house, which I do believe is closer to the village, mother." He smiled as he continued, "Should you wish to remain, you will remove yourself there post-haste and not return to this house until I give you leave to do so. Otherwise, you will return to London this day."

"That dower house is a morgue!" Came the snide reply, "Besides, I cannot return to London as both you and your chit have taken the carriages."

"There are these marvellous things known as stage coaches, mother."

Before the woman could utter any more protests, Xander rose and left the room to ready himself for travel.

One thought now dominated his mind: He would fetch back his wife and they would deal with whatever problems she had once and for all!

Chapter Twenty-Two

It took four days for Connie to reach Hague House. During that period, the driver and footmen who accompanied her obtained her unwavering devotion. To be truthful they had gained it the very first day when, upon arrived at an inn to feed the horses, they arranged for her to have a bath and hot meal readied for her and she was touched to find a pair of fine walking shoes waiting in the carriage upon her return.

In return for their kindness, Connie had insisted that the men dine with her at each meal, she had to persuade them to do so by saying it was for her protection. She also requested each night that the men have the finest available rooms. Connie did not care that their comfort exceeded hers, she had forced them to make the rushed, impromptu trip after all!

Her arrival at Hague House was met with much less chaos than she had anticipated. Fortunately, the only member of her family in the house was her mother as her father and brothers were off visiting with the tenants and Jane had opted to visit with her sister before joining the rest of the family.

Cora greeted her daughter with a worried look on her face and escorted her daughter to her private drawing room.

Once she had ensured they had enough tea and biscuits to last several hours, Cora dismissed the servants and patiently waited for Connie to explain.

Connie did not hesitate; she recounted every moment since her first meetings with both Xander and the Dowager Countess. Divulging through tear-filled eyes how she had come to feel so alone, helpless, and humiliated.

Once she had finished her sorry tale, Connie wiped away the rest of her tears and looked to her mother, anxiously awaiting the reprimand she surely deserved for being so foolish.

Instead, to Connie's surprise, the Duchess raised her hand to cup her daughter's cheek and her mouth lifted into a sad smile as she said, "My sweet, I am so sorry that I failed to prepare you to face how cruel this world can be."

Connie was astonished. If there was one belief, she had held in her entire life that would be unwavering, it was that her parents had been the most perfect parents she could ever had hoped for. She was raised in a house filled with love and affection and never felt as though she wanted for anything. Why would her mother think she had failed?

"Mama, never apologise for the fact that you have been the most wonderful mother to have ever lived."

Cora softly laughed as she met her daughter's eyes. "I could have done a much better job at lowering your expectations, I think." Connie grasped her mother's hands to squeeze. "I know how lucky I am. I have a husband whom I love, four wonderful children and a life where I have never wanted for anything. Sometimes, I feel, when one has only ever known joy, they have no clue how to handle sadness."

Cora's words gave Connie pause to consider their merit. Her mother was correct in saying that Connie had never had to deal with so many negative emotions as she had now. Yes, there were tiffs with her brothers, but they were simple sibling bouts. She excelled in all her lessons, even without Xander, her first London season had resulted in an almost immediate engagement. Even now, as hard as the other problems were, she was a countess and already expecting her first child.

Connie realised that she had never truly suffered through failure or emotional distress in her life. And, in the past few months, she had dealt with many and had no idea whatsoever on how to handle it.

Taking a deep breath, she turned her maze back to her mother and asked the only question that felt right in that moment: "How can I learn to handle my problems?"

On the outset it seemed a silly question, but Connie needed to know so that next time, instead of running miles away to her parents, she could face her problems head-on.

"Unfortunately, my sweet, life's problems are not mathematical equations and so there is no easy answer." Cora said, "What we do is we look at a problem and try to fix it."

"Mama that is the most ina......"

"And if we succeed in our methods, we know next time how to approach that particular problem. And if we fail in our methods, we dust ourselves off, remind ourselves not to do that again and try something else."

"Trial and error then?"

"If there were an easy answer, I would give it to you in a heartbeat. But there is no easy answer in life, all we can learn to do is live it our own way and hope for the best!"

Connie sighed, realising for the first time her mama would not be able to solve her problems for her.

"I somehow do not think trial and error is going to help with a murderous mother-in-law though." She lamented.

"Now that I will solve for you," Cora's tone was reproaching, "Helena Chalmers may be frivolous and vain, but she is not stupid enough to commit murder and risk alienating an important ducal family."

Connie rubbed her hands over her face as she processed her mother's words. "Oh god, she must be laughing at me as we speak! I genuinely believed her and ran away. Of course, she's going to be steadfast in her view of me after doing *that*."

She looked up to see her mother desperately trying (and failing) to stifle laughter. Connie could not help but join her mother and soon the room was filled with the sound of their unbecoming cackles.

Once they had gathered their wits, Cora helped her daughter to her feet, put her arm around her and led her out of the room.

"I will say, however, that whilst you are under my roof, I can solve some problems for you." Cora stated, "I have already ordered your room prepared. You are going to go upstairs and rest. I will arrange for some of my dresses to be taken to your rooms, luckily you are not showing yet. Then you will dress and join us for dinner where we will take much joy in pestering Duncan over how he should be married next."

Connie took her leave of her mother and made her way to her childhood bedroom. She gladly sank into the pillows and found herself indulging in the most peaceful sleep she had had since before she met Alexander Chalmers.

Well rested and dressed in a yellow chiffon dress from her mother's wardrobe, Connie ventured into the parlour of Hague House, where she was met with confused stares from her two eldest brothers.

"I thought we were rid of her." Duncan's remark was met by a clip around the ear from their father.

Taking a seat, Connie answered back, "I feel obliged to tell you, undearest brother, that as a married woman I am free to come and go as I like now."

"And make up new words, it appears." Matt commented, sipping his brandy.

James Wexford bent to kiss his daughter on the cheek before moving to stand by the fireplace. "I must say, Constance, when your mother told me you had arrived, I was rather worried but taking a look at you it appears my fears were unfounded."

"Not unfounded, Papa, just well rested and soothed by my mother's words of wisdom." Connie beamed up at her father.

"Yes, Mama did say you looked rather haggard when you arrived." Matt contributed, to which Connie poked her tongue out at him in response.

"You knew as well?" Duncan was clearly exasperated, "Am I the last one to be told anything?"

"Well, I am fairly certain Harry does not know yet." Connie teased.

"That does not count, Harry is in Denmark." Three heads tilted in confusion at Duncan's assertion.

"And why would our brother, a lieutenant in the British Army fighting in the French Wars, be in *Denmark?*" Matt queried.

Duncan shrugged, "Whoring, perhaps."

"He's making me prouder than you at this time, I'll say that!" came the scathing response from their father.

"Or he could be regaling the entire Danish court with the tale of when he had constructed that long trail of gunpowder along the Epsom racecourse and........."

"Oh, will you ever stop needing to tell *that* story?" Cora remarked upon entering the room. Walking over to the chaise currently seating her middle son, she shoved his legs onto the floor and took the seat in their place.

"Two things, Mama," Duncan responded, "Firstly, any sport where animals can be brutally killed, I hate, so that story brings untold legions of joy to me. Secondly, you could have asked for me to move my feet."

"Connie, darling, did you sleep well?" Cora ignored her son.

"Oh yes, Mama, I forgot how wonderful that bed is."

Matt sniggered before contributing, "I am sure your husband will love it as well, where is the Earl might I ask?"

Connie opened her mouth to respond but a deep voice coming from the doorway prevented her.

"Right here," Connie paled. "I would have come down sooner, but I must say this house has far more staircases than I was prepared for."

The seat next to her dipped and lips grazed Connie's cheek as her husband joined her. She remained seated in silent shock as her husband exchanged pleasantries with her family.

When dinner was announced, she allowed Xander to take her arm and escort her into the dining hall. Connie was dismayed to find herself sat across from her husband and was forced to avoid his intense gaze throughout all four courses.

It did not take long, Connie supposed, for her family to realise that something was amiss. Curious glances were directed to her as her contributions to the discussion were uncharacteristically minimal.

Her brain was abuzz as she wondered why her husband had followed her across the country. After their last debate he had ceased all meaningful contact, not even coming to her bed at night.

Fear washed through her as she considered the possibility that the Dowager Countess had informed her son that his wife had beaten her and run away. Knowing the woman, Connie would not be surprised if she had grossly exaggerated the tale. Could Xander have followed her to enact punishment for her actions?

On the other hand, Connie was carrying his child. Perhaps he simply wished to be there should any troubles arise.

Whatever her husband's motivations were, the fact remained that he was currently sat in her parents dining hall and, unless Connie somehow managed to hide from him the entire visit, would soon be confronting his runaway wife for her behaviour.

Connie was relieved by the brief respite allotted to her when the men and women parted briefly following the meal. Her father insisted on sharing his cigars with the men whilst her mother insisted they smoke them on the terrace as the smell disagreed with her.

Returning to the parlour, Connie allowed her mother to hand her a glass of claret before directing a stern expression to the older woman.

"Explain."

"Connie, sweet, did you honestly not think he might follow you?"

"I am not asking after his actions, Mama."

Her mother became somewhat flustered. "My actions? What am I supposed to have done? Turned the man away from the door?"

Connie's gaze was unwavering, "You were supposed to warn me that he had arrived."

"Yes, well I clearly did not have the chance."

"You could have told me before I left my room, woken me up before that. Honestly, Mama, I would have been grateful if you had even announced to all of us that he was here rather than leave me so surprised."

Cora opened her mouth to respond before changing her mind and closing it again. She took a sip of her wine and Connie heard a muffled apology come from her mother's lips.

She would forgive her in the morning, she decided, at the current moment she was too tense to even consider it.

The pair sat in an awkward silence until they heard the men making their way into the room, to which the women responded to by suddenly beginning an animated discussion over baby names to disguise the tenseness.

Connie was discerned when her husband chose to stand by her side, casually resting his arm over the back of her chair.

Deciding to make up for her lacklustre participation during dinner, she attempted to keep up with the animated debate her brothers were engaged in over how many kings they believe committed nepoticide.

All attempts of focus, however, went out the window when she felt a finger drift up and down the back of her neck. Goosebumps erupted all over her body and desire shot straight to her womanhood at the first affectionate touch from her husband in weeks.

Her lust grew even further when her husband leant down and spoke faintly so no one else could hear.

"What am I going to do with you? I should take you across my knee for the fright you gave me, *wife*."

Connie's breath hitched at his words, she found herself unable to respond as she felt herself melting in his presence.

"I spoke truly when I said I wanted no other woman but you, Constance. So, as you can imagine, the lack of rutting these past few weeks has left me rather frustrated."

Her only response was a small squeak. "I am afraid I did insist that we would prefer I join you in your room rather than have another needlessly prepared".

"I tell you, wife, I am going to be positively primitive when we retire tonight. Do you understand?"

Once Connie nodded in understanding, Xander straightened back up and joined in on the fervent debate.

She, on the other hand, gave up all hope of making any contributions to the conversation. Her mind was instead overrun with images of her husband, naked, with her hips in his hands as he ruthlessly pounded into her. Her desire was so strong that she feared she would stain the seat below her.

Giving up all pretence of wanting to be in company, Connie bade her goodbyes and returned to her bedroom, where she was pleased to find her ladies maid waiting for her, having been brought to Gloucestershire by her husband.

Dismissing the girl once she had been dressed for bed, Connie lay atop the covers and ran her hands over her body, eagerly anticipating her husband soon joining her.

Impatient for the impending pleasure, her hands drifted lower to play with her sex. When her husband finally did arrive, several minutes later, it was the dark look of lust in his eyes that tipped her over the edge.

When Xander allowed Connie to sleep, hours later, she felt the most sated she had been in a long while and the next day, Connie was surprised to find herself proud rather than embarrassed over the fact that she had found herself unable to walk properly.

Chapter Twenty-Three

Connie looked so serene as she slept that Xander chose not to wake her and dressed and left the room as stealthily as he could.

He was met on his way to breakfast by Duncan, who acknowledged his presence by wordlessly gesturing his head towards the entrance doors. When Xander queried if he intended for them to miss breakfast, an apple was suddenly thrown at his head in response.

Regaining his senses, he jogged to catch up with his brother-in-law. They spent several moments in silence, simply observing the early morning glow on the gardens.

Duncan led the pair down a gravel path through the surrounding woods until they reached a glistening lake. Duncan picked a pebble off the ground and threw it into the lake, making it bounced thrice before it disappeared into the rippling waters.

"Embarrassingly, that is the best I can manage." Xander managed five bounces on his first attempt. "You should challenge Connie. She always outdid us brothers."

Laura Osborne

Xander chortled, "Connie being the best at something? I'm not sure I believe you." Duncan smiled as he picked up another stone, judging the weight.

"Do you know what it is like to have a sister, Sutton?"

"Only brothers, unfortunately."

"Count yourself lucky, I have a brother currently in the middle of a war and I still worry for my sister more." The younger man's brow furrowed. "I suppose that says quite a bit about me?"

"That you love your sister?"

"I'd kill for her you know. Matt and Harry would too but Connie and I have always shared a special bond, which makes me far more protective of her."

"She's very lucky to have you." Came Xander's reply to which Duncan hurled his stone at the water.

"Then you can only imagine what it is like to hear what feels like everyone in London gossiping about her." His eyes were staring daggers. "Every moment I was in that godforsaken city I heard countless tales of how miserable her life was."

Xander sheepishly nodded, having been subject of the gossip himself. "So, tell me what the bloody hell is going on man? One minute she was blissfully happy and glowed everywhere she went then out of nowhere my sister turned into the biggest drip I have ever encountered."

Xander rubbed the back of his neck as he considered how to respond. It came to him that this was the very conversation Larry had suggested he needed to engage in, he just needed to work up the nerve to come out with it.

"Well, we had a bit of a disagreement when she told me she was with child," Xander picked up a stone that he suddenly became fascinated with tracing its shape. "And I fear our difference of opinion is only going to get worse as time goes on."

He glanced up to find the other man staring at him, unblinking. "Well, the sooner you tell me what it is, the sooner we can fix it man?"

"You won't like it......oh hell, I don't suppose I care any more about pleasing everyone." Xander rued. "Whether you Wexford's like it or not, I am and shall remain on the best terms with the Ainsworth family."

"Nobody's perfect, I suppose." Came Duncan's sardonic reply, which Xander could not help but laugh at.

"So, we come to an impasse, I won't give up the people who family who care for me far more than my own and Connie refuses to give them a chance."

"I can't blame her."

"I do not care if you approve of her choice or not, every time the family is mentioned she lashes out in an unreasonable manner."

Duncan's hands went to his pockets as he kicked a pebble. "It is not *that* unreasonable I think."

"Oh, then please enlighten me as to why." Xander's voice rose. "Even the bloody Ainsworth family has no clue as to why you lot are so hostile to them."

Duncan raised his hands in mock surrender. "Look, I don't know most of them, so I cannot make any claims of their character at all. What I do know is that old Ainsworth is not the kind of man you would wish to leave with anything you care about, especially if thing is a.........*young woman.*"

"A young woman?" Xander could not believe what he was hearing. "You are telling me that you lot have chosen to ostracise an entire family because Geoffrey Ainsworth seduced someone?"

"I would not say seduced exactly," Duncan sucked in a breath, "that suggests that the lady in question was willing."

Xander froze at the words, shock overcoming his features. "*That* is a very serious accusation you're making."

"I wish I did not have to make it but unfortunately I do."

"Look here, I know old Ainsworth has a reputation with the ladies, but I have never heard of it have any nefarious involvements."

Duncan rolled his eyes. "Perhaps he ensures he is on his best behaviour with the ladies of the Ton."

Xander crossed his arms in disbelief prompting Duncan to throw his hands in the air in exasperation. "Look, you can choose to believe me or not. I have it on good authority that he has done this on at least one occasion and the rest of the family, including your wife, believe it to be true. Now you have the reason why Connie is behaving as she is, and you can do whatever you wish with it."

The man began to stomp back up the gravel path before halting abruptly and turning to face his brother-in-law. "Whatever choice you make, try to pick one that makes my sister happy."

Xander watched Duncan's retreating figure. He could not believe what the man had told him. Geoffrey Ainsworth a.......a....... he could not even bear to think of the word.

Yes, the man was rather vocal in getting his own way and had a reputation for brutishness so large that it was often joked upon by his children. But this was something else.

Still, it explained Connie's behaviour these past months. Thinking back to the only occasion he could recall seeing the pair together, Xander had thought it odd at the time how Connie's demeanour had become so guarded in an instant. No wonder if she thought the man capable of......*that*.

No wonder she was so adamant overstaying away from the family. This was much worse than he could ever have anticipated.

Xander yelled into the air before briefly keeling over. Letting out an irritated breath, he turned away from the lake and march back up the path to the house.

As the house came back into view, he found his footsteps faltering. Coming to a standstill, Xander decided a change to tact might be to his advantage.

Changing his destination, he walked to the stables to order a horse saddled. Xander was going to get to the bottom of this today!

Twenty-seven miles and a little under an hour later, Xander brought his horse to a stop, dismounted, and handed the reins to a stable boy.

He stormed through the doors of Ainsley Manor and navigated his way to the breakfast room, where five pairs of eyes turned to him in shock. Ignoring the stares, he helped himself to a plate of food before taking a seat next to Marie.

After a beat of silence, Freddie turned to his mother and asked, "Must we go to this dinner tonight?"

His words broke the spell of silence in the room and regular morning chatter resumed as if Xander had not just unexpectedly appeared out of nowhere.

Chewing on a piece of bacon, he glanced up at Liam, who remained the only one looking quizzingly at him. Tilting his head, his expression appeared to ask if he was alright. Xander gave a small shake of the head in response to which his friend nodded in understanding.

Looking around the breakfast table, Xander wondered how the wonderful, animated people that surrounded him could possible be harbouring a man capable of such horrific acts.

They must have no idea, Xander surmised.

Once breakfast had concluded, each Ainsworth left the table one by one until only Liam remained. Verity was the only member of the family to acknowledge the surprise appearance, gently resting her hand upon Xander's shoulder before departing the room.

The two men sat in silence for a moment, the only noises permeating through the room being the sounds of their teacups as they were lifted, drained and put down.

It was the Ainsworth who broke the calm.

"I gather it would be superfluous to ask if you are alright." A low chuckle left Xander's throat as he looked at his friend. He stood to softly close the door, giving them privacy, before returning to his seat. He placed his elbows on the table, interlocking his fingers as he prepared himself.

"I need to know exactly what you believe your father to be capable of."

Liam's nose crinkled in bewilderment. "My father? What does my father have to do with anything?"

"It has come to my attention that certain people believe he is capable of committing particular heinous acts."

"Those people having the name 'Wexford' I assume?" Xander nodded in assent. "Look, I have no clue what they are suggesting but I doubt he could do anything that bad."

"Including rape?" Xander blanched at having to say the word aloud.

"Dear god, you must be joking!" *I wish I were.*

Xander rubbed his hand over his eyes, "You know I consider you all to be family, in fact, there is only one person in this world whom I love as much as you all. But I can see how others could believe it." Liam stood to pace the room in frustration.

"You can believe it? Don't you dare do this, Sutton! Do not push away the people that love you because of a silly rumour."

"I am not saying that I believe it!" Xander defended himself, "Your father puts on a mask when in society, they have no clue as to how kind and funny he can be. Jesus Liam, it took years for me to even see it!"

"So, what do you suggest, *friend*?" Xander flinched at the bitterness in his friend's voice.

"I'm going to speak to Connie, I do not think I can convince her to change her mind, but I believe I can convince her to at least give the rest of you a chance."

"You expect me to play host to that......"

"I am asking if you would consider showing my wife the kindness that I know you all have." Liam's only response was to balk and roll his eyes. "Please, Liam, if I cannot convince either of you to try, I will have to choose."

Liam turned his back and looked out the window, unresponsive.

"I will not be my father, if I have to make the choice, Connie and the baby will always come first." Xander stared at the back of his friend's head as he pleaded. "I am doing all I can to not lose the people I love. Please help me."

Minutes ticked by as the room was enveloped in silence. Worry dogged Xander's features as he began to contemplate what a life without his friend would look like. What would it mean for Calvert? The third member of their trio had no clue as to the stalemate that was currently taking place.

"Losing you would mean losing a piece of myself, you know." Liam's voice brought his friend out of his imagination. He turned, looking serious. "And I know my mother's heart would break. I cannot imagine what it would be like to see you in society and not be able to go and joke with you."

Xander swallowed at the thought.

"I am sure that if she truly believes that my father........." Liam's voice trailed off, clearly unable to form the words.

"It will be because her family has convinced her so."

"Yes, well.......even if she thinks so, she can say nothing to the rest of the family. I do not wish to deal with the upset it could cause."

"Connie is naïve, not stupid Liam. She'll know not to bring it up." Liam nodded in agreement as relief washed over Xander.

"My father will not be returning for another two weeks; I shall speak with my mother and send an invitation to dinner before then."

"Thank you." Liam's gaze hardened as he spoke, "I am doing this because you are my brother and I refuse to put myself and my family through the distress of losing you. I have no loyalty to your wife and refuse to pander to her."

"Have no fear," Xander laughed, "I will do the pandering and ensure that she will be on her best behaviour."

Nodding his head, Liam began to crack his knuckles, "Good to hear, now get out of here. I feel the need to hit something, and you do not want to be close when I do so."

Xander rose and walked to his friend. Shaking his hand in thanks, he took his leave. Stopping in the drawing room on his way out, he then gave his thanks to Verity for the meal.

Fetching his horse, Xander mounted and began the return journey to Hague House at a leisurely pace. He felt more positive by the moment as he thought *One down, one to go!*

Chapter Twenty-Four

Connie basked in the warm rays of the sun as she lay sprawled on the grass, her eyes closed as the sounds of her brothers sparring echoed throughout the grounds.

She had been disappointed to awake and find her husbands side of the bed cold and empty and was even more disappointed when she was told of his leaving the house early in the morning.

She had spent the day lounging, having discovered when she made her way to breakfast that she was unable to walk without experiencing jolts of pain. Although Connie was sure her mother would chastise her for spending too long in the sun, she simply did not care.

Lying back, a small smile framed Connie's face as she gently caressed the small bump that was beginning to form, hinting at her condition. Her smile turned to a frown, however, when she felt a cool shadow block the sun's rays.

Opening her eyes and blinking several times to adjust to the brightness, the smile returned when she saw the figure of her husband looking down at her. Gesturing to her side, she silently beckoned him to join her on the grass, to which he obliged.

Xander had opted not to lay down, instead sat with one leg sprawled in front of him and the other bent so that he could rest an arm on his knee. Connie turned to lay on her side, looking up at his face, which appeared serious in contemplation.

"I should chastise you, you know," Connie said, hoping to lift the mood, "I could barely walk when I rose this morning."

His eyebrows perked up in curiosity before furrowing as worry etched his features. "I'm sorry, flower, I should have been more gentle, considering your condition."

Connie laughed, "I was rather surprised at your.…...aggressiveness.…...I suppose it was to punish me for taking off at first light."

"More like punishing you for daring to touch what is mine." Connie quivered at his words.

"I had become so frustrated waiting for you that I decided to start without you." Her eyes met his in challenge as his thumb began to tenderly trace her lips.

"I'd rather you didn't, it's a bit embarrassing really, you having to do my job for me."

"Alright, if you insist, I shall refrain from touching myself again." Connie said, "But you ought to prepare yourself for I shall have to seek you out at any hour of the day to obtain my pleasure."

"Luckily for you I cannot seem to find even a hint of a suggestion that I can resist your body." Xander's head ducked as he planted the barest of kisses upon her lips.

Straightening again, he watched Matt and Duncan as he spoke. "We do need to sort this out though, Connie."

"Sort what out?" He flashed her a look of disbelief.

"You know exactly of what I speak." A chill ran down Connie's spine at the thought. She knew he was going to try again but she refused to allow herself any contact with *that man*.

Thinking quickly, Connie realised she had one form of distraction that would easily gain his attention, in addition to being another thing that would need to be discussed.

"Oh of course, I suppose we do need to take further steps now that your mother has decided to go beyond petty insults."

"For the love of.........what has she done now?" Connie found herself unconsciously shrinking into herself as she realised the weight of what she was about to say.

"She sort of made a comment about wishing our child to either die or come out deformed."

"WHAT?!" She looked upwards to find her husband looking at her with shock horror on his face. Before she could speak further, she found herself jolted up as he held onto her arms and lifted her, so their eyes were level with one another.

"Constance, explain yourself right now."

"Just breath darling." Connie tried to soothe him. "I know now she was not serious, but I was rather frightened at the time."

"What on earth would have compelled the woman to make a comment like that to begin with?" He still held her arms in a death grip.

"She was angry that I refused to remove myself from the countess' bedchamber and decided to blurt any many hurtful things."

"I suppose this was the moment when you slapped and shoved her to the ground?"

Connie giggled and felt his grip loosen, allowing her to lift her arms to wrap around his neck. "I am afraid so." She gently tugged his neck so that their lips met in a kiss.

"I don't think I've ever been more aroused in my life." Xander mumbled against her lips, kissing her once more.

His hand cupped the side of her jaw as she probed his lips with her tongue, obtaining entry. A low moan emitted from his throat, which quickly turned to a growl as they were disturbed by the shouts of her brothers, pleading with them to stop.

Flashing the pair a taunting look, Connie grabbed Xander's hand and pulled him up with her, immediately dragging him to the house.

"Connie, slow down." Xander stalled in his steps as they reached the terrace as he pulled her to face him. They took a moment to catch their breath, Connie bit her lip as the lust continued to rise in her.

"Please take me to bed, I need you inside me." She observed the movements of his throat as he swallowed in response.

"I think it was you taking me to bed." A strained smile crept across his lips. "But we must stop tumbling to the sheets whenever we have a problem. Connie, even if her words were empty, they were still threatening. I cannot allow these issues with my mother to continue."

"What can we do, though? She does not listen to reason and any conversation evolves into theatrics as she throws a tantrum."

"I told her she wasn't allowed in the house again." Connie was rendered speechless at his words. "She was given the choice to move her things to the dower house or to return to London."

She struggled to comprehend his meaning, surely it would not be so easy to get rid of the woman.

Not wanting to lift her hopes up, she cautiously asked, "What should happen when we are all in London?"

"I shall find alternative housing arrangements for her."

"Surely you do not think to support two separate households? Think of the cost." Connie urged, to which his eyes glistened, and a booming laugh left his lips.

"Flower, you do realise your husband is one of the richest men in England do you not?"

Connie's cheeks reddened as she remembered how truly wealthy he was, of course he would have no trouble supporting an additional household, he would support ten more if he wished to.

"Well, I suppose that is one problem we have solved without needing to go to bed." They shyly smiled at one another.

"Yes, one problem. But we do have others." Realising that her earlier diversion tactic was now returning to the original conversation, Connie tried her hand at another.

Reaching for his hand, she pulled him into the house and wandered along the hallway until they reached the entrance to the orangery. Peering inside, she found the room unoccupied and unceremoniously shoved Xander in the room before her.

"Connie, what are you up to?" came the suspicious words from his lips.

Letting out a giggle, Connie brushed her hand along the plants as she sauntered over to him. She ignored him when he repeated the question and only met his eyes when she came to a halt before him.

Wordlessly, she dropped to his knees and began working the fastenings to his trousers. An intake of air was heard above her head and when she reached to release his manhood, all he appeared to be able to do was mutter her name.

Leaning forward, Connie lifted her eyes to meet his hooded ones and she licked him from base to tip. His eyes fluttered closed, and his hands found their way into her hair.

Uncaring to the sounds of the pins holding her curls in place dropping to the floor, Connie placed a kiss on his tip before drawing him into her mouth.

Starting slow, she took in more of his cock with each movement until she finally held the whole length of him in her mouth.

With one hand reaching behind him to clasp a cheek, she used to other to caress his balls. Spurred on by the groans coming from his throat, Connie sped the movements of her mouth, sucking his shaft as much as she possibly could.

She barely heard the sound of a plant pot crashing beside her as his hand crashed into it. All she could focus on was his cock in her mouth as she felt him begin to shudder. Needing him to find his release, Connie took his entire length in her mouth and began to swallow, letting the sensations of her throat close around him.

With a groan from his mouth, he pulsated, and Connie felt the stream of his release pour down her throat.

Wanting to prolong his pleasure, Connie began moving her head again, frantically bobbing up and down on him and moaning at the taste of him.

When there was nothing more left of his seed, Connie released his cock and moved to lick any residue remaining off him.

Hands suddenly pulled her back to her feet as lips came crashing against her own. She wrapped her arms about his neck and ran her hands through his hair as he tasted himself on her tongue.

Finally pulling apart, Connie licked her lips as her husband ran his eyes over her body.

"You look a mess." His voice was husky as he spoke. Connie took in his trussed hair and still exposed manhood as she returned the compliment.

With a hearty laugh, Xander pulled her back into his arms as he murmured, "What am I going to do with you, petal?"

"Take me to bed I hope." Connie sighed.

First draft

To my mother,

I have decided upon consultation with my wife that it would be best for you to find new permanent lodgings separate from our household. I will arrange a yearly allowance to provide for you. If you exceed the funds you shall have to find supplements elsewhere.

Second Draft

Dowager Countess,

I note that you refrained from advising me of the full circumstances of my wife's departure from the house. Having been enlightened regarding the threats you had made upon my wife and child I can no longer in good conscience allow you to remain in our household. I am sure you will be able to entreat upon your fellow society matrons for accommodation before finding a permanent residence.

Third Draft

Mother,

I have wondered recently, if there was anything that you could have done to give me any reason to harbour any love for you or choose you over my wife. It came to me that you had three and twenty years to offer any affection you could have held.

It strikes me that I have been spending my life both pushing away and seeking the love you did not hold for me elsewhere. I have therefore found myself enfolded in the warmth of two families not my own.

Although I have now found peace at the hurt I have endured, the thought that I could put my child through the same endurance fills me with horror. In a few short months I will be a father and I find that I cannot in good faith allow you to have unrestricted access to my child.

I am sorry that it had to be this way, but I will allow nothing to come before Connie and our child.

Fourth draft

Lady Mother,

I am in the process of arranging alternative housing for you upon your return to London. I wish you well.

Your Son,

Alexander Chalmers, Earl of Sutton

Chapter Twenty-Five

The days that followed seemed to Connie to be a repeat of the days immediately following their wedding. She and Xander took every opportunity to steal into darkened corners of the house to thoroughly reacquaint themselves with one another's bodies.

Much to her chagrin, the fact that they were currently residing at her parent's home prevented them from spending every minute alone together.

Connie was thrilled to find her husband warm and attentive, taking care to provide for all her wants and needs in her condition. Although it did lead her to wonder if his concerns would turn from sweet to stifling the further along in her pregnancy she became.

The pair were currently exiting the village church following the Sunday sermon with her family. Taking a moment to lift her face to the sun, she beamed with happiness and thanked God for all her current blessings.

She was drawn from her moment of peace by a gentle pull on her hand. She turned to find her father placing it in the crook of his elbow as he began to walk her back to their group, who had already begun to leisurely stroll back to the house.

Lifting her free hand to rub her father's arm, Connie beamed at the duke. "Is this not the loveliest day you have ever seen?"

"Perhaps it would have been if it were not a Sunday." Chuckling at his daughter's quizzical look, the duke explained, "The church was so stifling that I was afraid the vicar would mistake the excessive sweat on my brow for evidence of my sins."

The pair laughed as they continued on. Looking ahead, Connie saw that her husband was currently engaged in an animated discussion with Matt whilst her mama was no doubt harassing Duncan once again about finding a wife.

"I must confess," her father said, "when he came to ask for your hand, I was convinced it would be the worst marriage imaginable. Needless to say, I am pleased to have obviously been proven so wrong."

Connie pursed her lips as she considered his words, "Why did you allow the marriage then?" she enquired. "We both know that you could have found me a husband in an instant."

"Well, your mother and I assumed, correctly might I add, that you were with child by then. He would have found out and there was half a chance that he would have caused trouble."

"What kind of trouble would that be?"

"I thought that if he was anything like the man we now know him to be, he would be devastated at being unable to acknowledge his own child." Connie looked up to see her father's eyes darken as he continued, "If he had been a cruel man, he could have used it for his benefit. I think we would have all been in trouble if that had happened."

"So, the easiest course was to allow us to marry then," Connie pondered, "I suppose you were not entirely wrong in your worries. They should have just been directed to his mother instead."

Connie jumped as her father's head fell back and he howled with laughter, drawing the attention of the rest of their party.

"I say, Connie, why are you never that funny with me?" Duncan teased, "It would have been nice to have a sister who is not boring."

Connie rolled her eyes as Cora lightly slapped his arm to scold him. She turned to see her father wiping tears from his eyes before escorting her to close the distance to the rest of the family.

"Trust me, I said nothing to warrant *that* as a reaction." She grimaced at her father before moving to hit Duncan's other arm herself.

"Oh yes you did!" The duke patted Xander's shoulder as he spoke to the man, "She just reminded me of what a lovely woman your mother is."

Suspicious confusion crossed her husband's features as he looked between the two of them.

"Oh please, do not start that again James." Cora begged of her husband.

"Do I want to know?" Matt asked.

"Did you know, Sutton, that many years ago I almost married your mother?" Both Connie and Xander's jaws dropped at the duke's question.

They stood still in surprise for a moment before moving quickly to join the party, who had resumed the walk home.

"Explain! Now!" Connie said.

Her father sniggered before he began his explanation. "Well, when I was a young lad, I had several unmarried ladies of the Ton trying to catch my eye. However, there were only two women I seriously considered."

Turning to his wife, softly caressing her hand that was placed upon his arm, he continued. "Now, one of these young ladies was perhaps the most beautiful woman I had ever laid eyes upon. Her eyes sparkled and my heart fluttered every time I spoke to her. She took more of my breath away with each passing day."

His head turned to meet his children's eyes, "And the other woman was your mother."

The joke earned him a slap on the arm from his wife whilst Duncan's responding laughter earnt him his third hit of the day from Matt. Connie considered asking her husband to administer the next inevitable blow so that he would have the entire Wexford set.

"Will you be serious James!" Cora chided.

"Oh fine," the duke pouted, "I wished to marry your mother as I was tricked into falling in love with her. *Ouch!* In the meantime, my father wanted me to marry Lady Helena as it would unite us with an old family, something us Wexford's had yet to achieve."

"You seriously considered marrying my mother?" Xander queried. "You know she's a harridan of the highest order, do you not?"

"She could have fooled me," came her father's reply, "she was rather good at hiding her true colours until after she landed herself a husband. My commiserations to your father for that one."

"How did you end up marrying Mama then?" Matt asked his father.

"Two things really. First, I had a hint of her true self when she *accidentally* knocked an entire bowl of lemonade onto your Aunt Patricia, not realising that she was courting William rather than I."

Connie saw her husband rub his hand over his eyes as he grimaced over his mother's behaviour.

"Of course, that first point did not matter to my father, so it was the second that was the deciding matter."

"And that was?"

"He dropped dead in the middle of an engagement ball hosted by the O'Neill's." Connie shivered at his words.

"Hold on," Duncan spoke, "I was under the impression that Grandfather's death was due to a battle injury."

"Yes, that was what the Ton joked about him. He was rather a boor and they rather enjoyed using the play on words to laugh at him."

"What was the play on words then?"

"His battle with the drink." Connie was surprised to see her father nodding in such a matter-of-fact manner. "The man was a drunkard and that night his heart could take no more. Or was it his liver? I do not know I am not a doctor. The point is, that the man was the only supporter of Lady Helena. After he died, I was able to marry the woman I loved.........and I've regretted it ever since."

"PAPA!"

"Honestly, James."

"Good god, you sounded convincingly sincere."

THUMP

Connie's wish came true.............Duncan had now been hit by everyone currently in his presence in response to his laughter.

The family continued on the path, relaxing into jovial debates over what life would have been like had the patriarch selected a different bride. Luckily, everyone was in agreement that the correct choice had been made.

Xander stood in silence, not even daring to take a breath, wary of disrupting the beauty of his wife gazing out the windows to the stars.

She had disappeared after dinner, claiming the pregnancy had made her weary, but Xander was surprised to find the bed undisturbed when he ventured to their room to see her.

Searching the house, he found her in a portrait gallery and, upon seeing his wife's position at the windows, was struck by the memory of the first time her had seen her.

Warmth flooded his body as he leant against the doorway watching.

After several moments of tranquil silence, his wife's back stiffened and she turned to finally see him. A smile graced her lips as she silently beckoned him over.

Wordlessly, Xander sauntered over and placed himself against Connie's back, wrapping his arms around her and resting his head beside hers as the pair turned their gazes outward. They were both content to take a moment to simply enjoy being in one another's company.

"Does this remind you of anything?" She huskily whispered. He responded with a low growl before turning his head slightly to nip her earlobe.

He almost came undone at the moan which emerged from her throat before forcing himself to snap out of it.

"I am afraid you will not like me very much tonight." He murmured.

"Hmmm?"

Reaching into his pocket, he retrieved the folded note that had been residing there for the past hour. Returning the arm to where it rested on her front, he gently unfolded the note and tilted it to allow his wife to read it in the light.

To no-one's surprise, Connie stiffened in his arms and attempted to push herself out of them. Refusing to avoid the conversation any longer, he kept them firmly in place.

"Connie, we have to discuss this sometime."

"This is not a discussion; it is a bombardment!"

"I think you are slightly exaggerating this, flower."

"Do not call me that whilst I am mad at you!" Her voice began to rise. "We were having a perfectly wonderful moment together before you forced *that* in my face."

"Heavens, who would have thought an invitation to dinner would be such a horror?"

Connie turned herself in his arms so that they faced one another. "You can go but I shall remain here."

"Connie..."

"I have made my position on the matter clear enough already."

"*Connie...*"

"I am not stopping you from any sort of a relationship, but I cannot be forced into going anywhere I do not wish to!"

"For the love of God, Constance, just because you believe the man to be a rapist does not mean that I do!"

Connie froze at his outburst, eyes widening. Xander took a moment to collect his thoughts, not wanting to cause any more trouble than he already had.

"Connie, these are people that I have known......."

"Let me go please." Xander refused to budge. "Ugh, if I promise not to leave the room will you release me?"

His hold on her loosened, allowing Connie to slip out and take several steps away before she turned back to face him. She appeared to be mustering all her courage.

"As I have said before, I will not prevent you from fostering any sort of a relationship with that family you wish to, but I shall not be a part of it!"

Xander crossed his arms as he leant against the wall beside the window and considered the best way to approach to matter with his wife.

"Constance, when your brother told me of your family's......belief......to say I was taken aback is putting it lightly. The Duke of Bristol is a man who has been kind to me for years and has taken on a fatherly role to me." He held his hand up to stop Connie when her mouth opened to interrupt. "Please, let me say my peace and then you can choose what course of action to take." She begrudgingly nodded in response.

"As I was saying, because of my relationship and knowledge of the man, I can scarcely believe what you and your family say is true. It gives me quite a conflict as your family have left me with the impression that they are all intelligent, level-headed people and honest. Therefore, I cannot imagine any of you would lie about this."

"But I also cannot believe that he would do something so terrible." Xander felt as though he could see his wife's heart break before his very eyes and his felt like breaking in response.

"I think we've reached a stalemate, petal. You say he did, I say he didn't, and I do not think either of us will change our minds anytime soon."

"So, what do we do now?" Connie asked, her voice shaking.

"I vote we do what any couple who desperately want to be happy together do," she tilted her head in confusion, "we compromise."

Biting her lip, Connie slowly made her way to Xander's side, where she placed her hands upon his shoulder and rested her chin upon them. He swallowed the groan that threatened to rise when he felt her front press into his side. It took everything in his power not to take her in his arms and end the conversation there and then.

"What is your proposal, my love?" Her soft voice made him turn his head towards her, smiling gently down to her.

"I never wish for you to be afraid, darling; I will never force you to spend any time in the company of a man who frightens you so." He felt her body soften as the tension left her.

"You will spend time with them on your own then? And not force me to endure their company?" Connie asked.

"No." Upon seeing the look of hurt cross her features, Xander hastily began to explain further, "Connie, I care more for that family than I do my own, except you, if you reject them all you will be rejecting a part of me."

"How do you expect me to spend time with them knowing what their father has done?"

"Because they do not know what is said of him. God, you should have seen the horror on Liam's face when I told him." Xander's head rested back against the wall as he remembered.

He looked down to see his wife's brow furrowed as she considered his request.

"Liam knows how important you are to me, and he only wants me to be happy so he has promised to ensure that any occasion to spend with the family will be in his father's absence."

Connie's eyes darted up in surprise at his words. "But just because they all love you does not mean that they will be kind to me. After all," Connie rolled her eyes as she continued, "this silly feud has been going on for almost a century."

Xander leaned his face towards hers with a glint in his eye, "Would you believe me if I told you they thought it even sillier?" He could not resist placing a light peck on her lips before he lifted his head again. He was overjoyed to see her smile for the first time in the discussion.

"You still do not even know if they will like me or I them."

"Actually, wife, I think you will find that they will like you because they know I adore you. Besides, you have already met Eliza and considering she is the reason why we are currently married so you must be grateful to her and if she gets to be too much, Marie is the perfect balance."

A dramatic sigh rolled off her lips as Connie acquiesced. "Very well then but if I am not convinced after this dinner then you will have to agree to reconsider your tactics."

Xander finally gave in and turned to wrap his arms around his wife. "Darling, you have no idea how happy you have just made me!" Connie sent him a mocking look in response.

"I do have to disagree on one thing you say, husband." Xander's head drew back in confusion. "Eliza Ainsworth is not the reason I married you and I can prove it!"

Connie rose to thoroughly kiss her husband before taking his hand and leading him to the door, presumably to escort him to their room.

Xander made a mental note to show her how thankful he was repeatedly once they reached their destination.

Chapter Twenty-Six

Connie was questioning for the fifteenth time this evening how she had allowed her husband to convince her to venture into 'the belly of the beast' as Duncan had oh so kindly called it.

The carriage journey to Ainsley Manor was largely spent in silence as any attempts made by Xander to begin conversation were met with unwomanly grunts and one-word responses. He eventually settled for gently rubbing the hand clasped in his, mildly alleviating Connie's nerves.

All progress he had made, however, was quickly scuppered upon their arrival into the entrance hall of the manor as directly overlooking the doors was a large portrait of the current Duke of Bristol. Shivers went down Connie's spine as she turned to her husband who, part of her was delighted to note, blanched at the sight. Whether because he saw it as a hindrance to his goal or some small part of him had an inkling that what had been said was true, Connie did not know. Either way, she decided, it brought some small comfort to her to see that her husband was not entirely unsympathetic and steadfast in his reconciliation attempts.

A gradual sense of ease fell upon her as the evening drew on. Connie could not find herself completely comfortable though, as the increasing winds and rain outside set her on edge and she could not help but notice that both Ainsworth men bore a glint of distrust and resentfulness in their eyes.

The seating arrangements additionally gave her little comfort. Although the party was small, making conversation less restricted allowing for the entire table to be involved, she still found herself feeling cut off from the security of her husband.

Sat at the head of the table was William Ainsworth, Connie had been placed on his left and his cousin, Marie, on his right. On the other end of the table, the Duchess was seated, with Xander on her right and her youngest son to her left. As luck would have it, rather than allowing for the married pair to be sat aside one another, thrust in the middle of the pair was Eliza, whom Connie was still entirely uncertain of. On one hand she had always shown her every kindness and had indeed facilitated Connie's marriage. But her outspokenness was entirely unusual for a Lady which made Connie feel rather out of sorts.

"You must tell me, My Lady, how are you not yet bored with my friend?" The young man on her right drew Connie's attention away from the pheasant on her plate.

"Bored? I do think you underestimate my husband's ability to hold one's interest, My Lord." Connie responded, earning a chuckle from the man.

"Perhaps, although I must admit in all the years I have known the man, I have never seen him hold attention for as long as he has had yours."

"He has maintained your attention for many years though, has he not?" Connie was surprised to see Ainsworth momentarily choke on his drink in shock at her words.

"Well, that's different," he sputtered out. "I am not a woman!"

"And any other woman you have seen him with before is not his wife, that is also different." She sent him a smile before taking a bite from her plate.

A giggle came from her left as Eliza joined in. "Well, well brother, I must say any person who can retaliate your attempts at teasing has approval in my book." Turning to Connie, she went on, "I do hope to see you more often, Connie dear, if just to make Liam feel more awkward than he usually does."

Connie could not prevent the small laugh that rose in her throat. "With three older brothers, I am afraid I had no choice but to learn the art of the rebuttal."

"If the other two are anything like the one I know, you definitely have your work cut out for you. How is Harry faring, by the way?" The sudden spark in Eliza's eye did not escape Connie, nor did the cough from Ainsworth which sounded an awful lot like "Lord Henry".

"Oh, Harry's well enough I suppose. His letters are showing his usual light-hearted self and he seems to be doing well in his commission." Connie's brows then furrowed in thought. "Although Duncan still remains rather adamant that he is in Denmark for some reason."

"Ah Denmark, that famous warzone." Lord Frederick's quip earned a murmur of laughter from the table.

"Wherever he is, we are all grateful for his service." The Duchess' dulcet voice said. "If God forbid you ever have any concerns for your brother, please do not hesitate to call on me. My sister, Mary, is married to General Cartwright, who works closely with Viscount Castlereagh. I am sure he can find out anything for you."

"I shall make note of that should I ever wish to commit treason, Mother." Liam quipped, making his mother shake her head in annoyance.

Pretending her son did not interrupt, the Duchess continued, "Even if it does not relate to your brother, I do hope that you find yourself able to come to us for help should you need it. Your husband is like a son to me, and I would take much joy in treating you the same."

As long as your husband is not involved!

Connie did feel guilty for the immediate thought that crossed her mind. For as horrific as she knew the duke to be, his family had done nothing but make a marvellous impression in her eyes and she was touched by the kindness of the Duchess.

"I must say, if our ancestors who had that dispute over that silly plot of land knew precisely how us Ainsworths had welcomed a Wexford into our midst, they would be turning in their graves!" Eliza pronounced.

"You only say silly plot of land because us Wexford's were the ones who ended up with it!" Connie spoke without thinking and stilled the moment the words left her lips. Silence fell over the room as every head at the table turned to hers.

Following a prolonged beat, laughter resounded through the air and Connie finally found herself truly at ease for the first time that evening.

Conversations began to spark up around the table. Connie observed Marie being teased by her youngest cousin and her husband had quickly turned red following a comment made by the Duchess, leaving her with her original two conversation partners.

A hand suddenly clasped around hers and squeezed. Eliza leaned forward to whisper to Connie. "I truly am happy to see you here, you mustn't think otherwise."

"If there is anything in this world I cannot doubt, Eliza, it is that you are sincere in your words." Connie squeezed her hand and smiled in response. Their hands released and returned to their meals as she continued. "If I am honest, it is slightly unnerving. I do not think I have met any lady in society who is as frank as you when she speaks. Publicly that is."

"I am turning prematurely grey as a result." The eldest Ainsworth contributed.

"I know most think it unbecoming," Eliza explained, "but with a Duke for a father, an exceedingly wealthy brother and an embarrassingly large dowry, I find I can get away with not being meek. And who am I not to take advantage of being able to behave as is my nature? We have to deal with enough restrictions as women so should be allowed whatever leeway's we can find."

Connie nodded in agreement at the other woman's words. Thinking back to the pressures she always had to be ladylike when she was a child, it was refreshing to realise the freedoms that certain privileges allowed her.

"I am afraid you shall have to get used to my sister's temperament, My Lady. She has been badgering Sutton to convince you to visit for so long that now she has you here, I fear she will not let you leave." A wicked glint crossed Lord Ainsworth's eyes as he spoke.

One part of his words grasped Connie's attention and she decided that now was as good a time as any to ask a question she had always wondered.

"I have noticed, My Lord, that whenever my husband speaks of you, he always uses your given name, but you do not do the same for him. Why is that?"

His head tilted in interest as he took in her words. "I think you are perhaps the first person to ask me that. Most people do not usually care."

"It is just rather odd." Connie said. "Etiquette says that you should be referred to by your subsidiary title, my eldest brother is. So, why is it that you are not called......?"

"Derry?" He finished her sentence for her. "I suppose it is somewhat like my sister finding her freedom where she can. It is rather stifling, you see, having a title that goes back to 1157 and a family history from even further." He absentmindedly twirled his fork in his plate as he spoke.

"For as long as I can remember, I have been called 'the future Duke of Bristol' or 'the eldest of the Ainsworths'. No one ever really cared about me as a person, I was always just an extension of my line. So, I decided that I wished for those who really knew me and cared for me would know me as simply Liam. Even for a short while I can be simply a man before the history books relegate me to just a title."

"It is adorable that you believe you will be in the history books, brother." He responded with a sad chuckle.

A wave of sympathy struck Connie. She had spent her entire life so in fear of this family that she did not take a moment to consider that they were, in fact, so alike her and her brothers. She made a mental note to apologise to her husband for failing to listen to his words about the people he loved. Especially in the case of the man currently sat beside her. Liam Ainsworth could have easily refused to allow Connie near his family for what she said about their father, regardless of the validity of the claims.

Deciding to lift the spirits, Connie spoke. "Do you know, for as long as I can remember I have been closest to Duncan, of all my brothers." Her companions looked at her in confusion. "One of the reasons why is that he was always the best at telling me stories and his favourite ones were the stories about your family."

Both Ainsworth's leaned back in their chairs in intrigue. "I was convinced that you all were green with tails and feasted upon little girls under the full moon."

The three all burst into laughter at the silliness of it all. Wiping the tears from her eyes, Eliza announced, "Have no fear, I can safely say none of those are true."

"I do not think we can honestly say that sister. You did have green hair a few years ago." Connie's head whipped round to question the lady on her left.

"Oh Liam, don't be cruel! How was I supposed to know that that witch was really a crazy woman?"

"Because we all warned you she was!"

Before Eliza could respond the room was lit up by a flash of lightning from outside. Everyone hushed as they looked to the windows and wondered when a storm had begun to rage.

"Oh dear," uttered the Duchess. Beckoning the butler over, she gave him orders to prepare a room for the night for Connie and Xander.

"Oh no, you do not have to do that." Connie's words rushed out of her mouth. Coming to dinner and getting to know the family was one thing but spending the night in the manor was quite another! Besides, knowing Connie's luck the duke would somehow find a way to return several days early.

"Connie, darling, I know you do not wish to be an imposition, but it is clearly not wise to even consider venturing out tonight."

"Nonsense, it is not *that* bad outside. We shall be in the carriage after all." Connie knew she was being ridiculous, but she did not have it in her heart to give up without somewhat of a fight.

In unison, the heads of all five Ainsworths turned to the windows, looked at the storm and turned back to look at Connie with faces that made her feel as though she had suddenly sprouted two heads.

"You are right, flower, we shall be fine in the carriage I imagine." Xander answered suspiciously. "Of course, the driver and footman shall both catch colds and die but that shall only matter to the families they will be leaving behind."

Feeling very much like a chastised child, Connie grumbled that she would stay. Discussion around the table resumed although Connie found herself once again on edge, ruing the storm having ruined the equilibrium that she had finally managed to obtain.

The rest of the evening went by without issue and Connie found herself escorted up to a room in the family quarters, much to her surprise. Her husband soon explained to her that it was his usual room in the house. It seemed Connie had underestimated exactly how much they treated him like family!

Settling in for the night, Connie having been lent a nightgown and change of clothes for the morning, she found her mind wandering to various scenarios where she would awake to find the duke returned and all protection faded away.

She jumped when a hand came to cup the side to her face and Connie turned her head to see her husband looking at her with concern. She then realised that her breathing was erratic, and she was trembling.

Without saying a word, Connie turned to her side and launched herself into Xander's embrace. Anchoring herself in his arms, she focused on the soft stroke of his hand on her back and fought to steady her breath. Gradually, her eyes grew heavy, and she fell into the depths of sleep. The last thought on her mind being the knowledge that, no matter what happened, if she was in Xander's arms, she felt safe.

Chapter Twenty-Seven

Connie knew she was being ridiculous. The storm raged all night, making the windows rattle and she could swear she heard the sounds of various paraphernalia outside being overturned. When she and Xander awoke and gazed out the windows in the morning, they jested that they had slept through a hurricane.

Despite this, when they ventured downstairs to break their fast, she still let out a sigh of relief when it had been confirmed that the duke had not returned home during the night. She had convinced herself that he would withstand the ruthless weather and travel solely to torment her.

She had then been able to relax herself and came to greatly enjoy the casual camaraderie at the breakfast table. She had expected the journey home to commence immediately following breakfast. These expectations were thwarted, however, when Xander agreed to assist the men in moving the fallen debris off the road. It appeared that there were several fallen trees blocking important routes for the farmers.

Seeming to sense that Connie felt somewhat out of sorts at the delay, Marie had asked if she would consider joining her in preparing baskets of emergency supplies for the villagers. Connie had gladly acquiesced and followed the older woman to the kitchens to beg cook for provisions.

Returning to the breakfast room, now cleared of food, and stocked with baskets and blankets, they set themselves to work.

After a few minutes of comfortable silence, Marie begun the conversation.

"I do hope you have not been feeling too put out by this visit, My Lady, I can imagine it has not been easy for you." Connie smiled at the considerate words.

"I confess, I did have more dread than anticipation once my husband informed me of your aunt's invitation. But having come here, I find myself far more at ease than I would have ever expected. And do please call me Connie."

"Only if you call me Marie." Came the sweet reply. "That is a relief to hear. I did worry that our family might frighten you away, we were all more informal than we would be when hosting guests."

"To my relief! If there is one thing, I loathe about society it is the stuffy politeness that must be conveyed at all times."

"If that is the only thing you find amiss with the Ton then I am jealous indeed." Marie giggled. "I would much prefer to stay home and tend to the garden than go to any event where I should be expected to smile prettily and find a stranger to marry!"

"I do not blame you. Had I not met my husband in such an.........*unorthodox* fashion, I would now be married to one of those strangers. I think I ended up with the better outcome."

"As I consider your husband to be a dear friend, I would have to agree." Marie nodded to emphasise her point.

"Do you find yourself in the gardens often?" Connie enquired.

"If the weather is well. I think Aunt Verity decided once I came to live with her that I would be her horticultural prodigy as a means of keeping me preoccupied. In addition to the fact that none of her children shared her passion for plants."

Her words gave Connie pause, she could not imagine what it would have been like for the young orphan, having her entire life uprooted to this grand house.

"How old were you when you came to live here?"

"I was two months shy of my fifth birthday."

"Was it difficult?"

The golden-haired woman bit her lip as she appeared to consider Connie's question. "I remember feeling safe with such a large, loving family determined to keep me happy and comfortable, considering the circumstances of my arrival. I remember Eliza had decided that I was there for her." Marie smiled at the memory. "Two years of age, she babbled more than talked and made me sleep in her little bed every night. Our governess was furious when she realised what was going on. I never used to mind though."

"I pestered my parents for years to give me a little sister." Connie said. "They told me they were trying but it never seemed to work out. And I have just realised what they meant when they said they were trying......I think I may be sick." Connie grimaced much to the other woman's amusement.

"You should have seen Eliza's face when she worked it all out. She was twelve and found a book in the library that explained it all. Naturally, she went and told the rest of us. Us three girls consider it a triumph how we did not give anything away when Aunt Verity sat us all down to explain it all when Colette was married."

The words prompted a round of giggles from the pair which were repeated as they bonded over various stories of their youths. Although it was unspoken, Connie formed the distinct impression that she and the quiet Ainsworth cousin had found themselves to be rather kindred spirits and she was surprised upon realising that she was eagerly anticipating when their paths would cross again in the future.

It took approximately three hours to sufficiently clear the roads enough for travel and Xander found himself greatly in need of a hot bath and a filling meal once they were done.

It was this that caused he and Connie to leave for Hague House seventeen hours later than they had intended when they had accepted the invitation.

Standing at the front of the house, making their goodbyes, Xander had to gather all his willpower to stop him bursting into a dance of victory upon observing Connie warmly bidding adieu to the Ainsworth women, embracing them, and clasping their hands as she spoke.

Just as wonderful was Liam giving a nod of approval and Freddie admitting that he found Connie most endearing. Although he did get in a crack that it was "in spite of her being a Wexford."

Settling into the carriage, facing his wife, Xander grinned smugly at her as she attempted to avoid meeting his eyes. Deciding to continue in his triumph, he sought to obtain her attention.

His first cough was ignored.

His second cough was ignored.

The gentle nudge of his foot against her resulted in his wife moving her legs away.

His exaggerated sigh received not a flicker of acknowledgement on her face.

Her eyes did not drift away from the window as he clapped his hands together thrice.

Having enough of her ignoring, Xander opted to go for more drastic means and promptly threw a cushion at her head.

Slowly turning her head to face him, her lips pursed, and eyebrows raised in annoyance, Connie finally spoke. "What?"

"Anything you have to say, petal?" He responded, smugly.

"Is there anything I should be saying?"

"Oh, I think you can figure out what would be best."

"Yes, I suppose you are right." Connie sighed. "I have been dreading this conversation but have it we must."

Xander was anticipating the gloating he would do as she continued.

"I think we should name our first son Humbert."

"Did I not tell you that you would enjoy……....*Humbert*?"

"It's divine, isn't it?" Connie beamed.

Xander could not believe what he was hearing. "I suppose when we're cooing at him, we'll call him Hummy?"

"Oh Hummy, how wonderful."

"Constance Chalmers, our child will be called Humbert over my dead body!"

"You are a spoilsport." Connie pouted. "Perhaps Hubert then?"

"Our child is not going to be named anything beginning with 'Hu' and ending with 'bert'."

"Alright then, might I suggest......"

"You are suggesting nothing, madam, as you are not going to be successful in distracting me." Xander pointed his finger at her. "Now admit you were wrong."

Connie's eyes narrowed at his order but quickly glistened as another scheme appeared to take place in her mind. Looking him dead in the eye, she began to remove each glove and untie her cloak.

Xander gulped and his voice was several octaves higher than normal as he asked, "What are you doing, Connie?"

"Admitting you are right, husband." She moved to the floor of the carriage to kneel between his legs.

"C...C...Connie?" He pulled at his collar, suddenly feeling rather restricted.

Taking his hand, she pointed to each finger as she spoke. "Now, there were five Ainsworths you conspired for me to interact with last night. Now let us consider the first."

She placed her fingers upon his thumb, brought it up to her mouth and proceeded to kiss, lick, and suck it as she spoke. "The Duchess is by far warmer and more maternal than I had anticipated. I was indeed rather touched at her offer to assist with Harry should the time arise."

Xander felt his mouth go dry as she moved to the next finger. "Liam Ainsworth is less harsh than I had imagined, and I find I understand why the pair of you are such good friends."

She took his middle finger into her mouth, swirling her tongue around the digit before releasing it with a *pop*.

"Of course, I was already acquainted with Eliza, but I was pleased to see that she was not as frivolous as I had previously supposed."

Xander did not know how she was able to make it to the fourth finger before he felt himself hardening.

"I think Marie is going to be the one I shall find myself the most endeared to. We seem to share many common interests and once you break through her quiet exterior, she is wonderful to converse with."

"Lord Frederick was polite for the little time we did speak." It appeared that would be all Connie would say regarding the gentleman, as she took his little finger and proceeded to draw the digit in and out of her mouth, mimicking the act she had become an expert pupil in learning.

With a groan, Xander used his free hand to palm him manhood through his trousers, desperately needing to find some form of relief.

Several moments later, Connie released the finger and moved his hand into a fist before placing light kisses upon his knuckles.

Finding his voice again, Xander said "You're not going to let me have my victory, are you?"

Connie nuzzled his hand and giggled before looking up to meet his gaze.

"Whatever makes you think that husband?" Gently placing his hand on his knee, she rose on to her knees and ran her fingers over his chest.

"You were right, and I was wrong, you are victorious, are you not?"

"Yes." He squeaked.

Connie licked her lips as her gaze turned lusty. "As a victor, you should have a prize." *Oh god* thought Xander.

Leaning to whisper in his ear, Connie uttered the words that almost made him spend himself in his trousers.

"How do you want me?"

Without missing a beat, Xander grasped her arms and pulled so that she straddled his thighs. Meeting her lips in a scorching kiss, Xander decided that this was going to be perhaps the greatest carriage ride of his life.

Chapter Twenty-Eight

Heat rose in Connie's cheeks after she exited the carriage with her husband and found her mother looking at their rumpled clothes in amusement. She sneaked a glace at Xander and scowled at the unaffected smug smile on his face.

After reassuring her mother that all had been well the night before and they had no troubles on their return journey, Connie made her way up to her room. She was stopped by her father and both brothers at various points and was made to repeat her assurances thrice, turning a five-minute walk into a twenty-five minute one.

Slipping into her bedroom, she kicked off her shoes in the most unladylike manner and then sat down at her dressing table and began to unpin and brush her hair.

Not two minutes had passed when Connie heard the bedroom door open and close. Looking up, she saw the reflection of her husband staring back at her. She shivered as she recognised the tell-tale lust in his eyes as he began to prowl towards her.

Coming to a stop at her back, he began to lazily unbutton her dress. Having freed successfully loosened the fabric, his fingertips began to lightly trace the edges of her bodice.

"That was most unfair of you in the carriage, Constance." Came his deep voice.

Leaning back against him, Connie gave herself in to the feeling of his fingers on her breasts as she breathlessly replied. "You cannot expect me to not use your weakness against you."

His head titled in interest before lowering so that his lips brushed her ear. "And what is my weakness, flower?" He nibbled at her earlobe as he waited for her reply.

"Me." She moaned; her eyes fluttering shut.

"Is that so?" His hands drifted lower to roll her hardened nipples between his fingers. "That cannot be fair that you know my weakness, but I do not know yours."

Connie's breathing grew heavy at his ministrations as she huskily replied. "You know you are my weakness, just as I am yours."

"I am, am I?" She felt his grin against her face. "So, you would not be able to resist me if I decided to have you? Wherever? Whenever?"

"Oh god Xander," she cried out when he pinched her nipple. "I am always yours for the taking."

"Will you ever say no to me Constance?"

"Never!" Her hips began to move in time with his fingers on her breasts. "I love you too much to deny you."

At those words, his hands stilled, and she could feel his sharp intake of breath upon her ear. Realising what she had said, her eyes darted open and met his widened ones in the mirror.

Connie felt as though their frozen state lasted forever as he processed her words. She could not believe they had slipped out of her mouth.

Finally moving, her husband kneeled by her side before turning her so that they faced one another. Cupping her face, his eyes appeared to search hers before he spoke.

"You love me?"

Finding herself suddenly unable to speak, Connie timidly nodded her head in confirmation.

"I need to hear you say it, flower."

"I love you." Her answer was barely a whisper.

Her heart leapt in joy as the brightest smile she had ever seen formed in his face.

"Say it again."

Her voice was louder this time. "I love you."

"Again."

"I love you."

"Again."

Laughing, she crushed her mouth to his, wrapping her arms around his neck and his came to rest on the small of her back.

Leaning her head back a touch, she looked him in the eyes and said "Alexander Chalmers, I love you. I think I've loved you for the longest time."

"I think I've loved you longer." Connie's vision began to blur as tears formed at his words. She did not know why she was so surprised that he felt the same. Perhaps it was some lingering remains of her initial guilt following their wedding. Perhaps it was her own insecurities. Whatever it was, it gave Connie what was perhaps the most wonderful surprise of her life.

"Do you really love me?" She beamed.

"Constance, you have amazed me with your kindness, your bravery and your spirit. You have faced off against my witch of a mother and allowed yourself to embrace those that I love the most despite it quite literally terrifying you. You risked scandal and ruin. And all of these you did for me. You gave me no choice but to love you."

The tears fell freely down Connie's face as she listened to his words. "Do you know that you can be a bumbling idiot at times?" He let out a hearty laugh in response. "I would do anything for you!"

His eyes became hooded as he leaned back onto his heels. "Then take your clothes off for me."

Connie felt her womanhood quiver at his words. Unsteadily rising onto her feet, her undone dress pooled at her feet. Not taking her eyes off her husbands, Connie gathered up the fabric of her shift and lifted it over her head, she then threw it to the side.

Raising her leg, she rested it against his chest as she used it as leverage to roll her stocking down. Tossing the piece of fabric behind her, she then repeated the process with the other leg.

Reaching down, she threaded her fingers through Xander's hair to pull him up so that he stood before her. Rising to give him a brief peck on the lips, she sat back on the stool, leaning back against the dressing table. Parting her legs, Connie ran her fingers through her moist folds and began to moan.

"Strip." She commanded.

Unlike Connie, Xander did not keep his eyes on hers. Instead, their gaze stayed unwavering on the movements of her fingers. She rolled her hips and felt her pleasure near as layer by layer, her husband's naked form was revealed before her.

Content to simply look at him, Connie rubbed circles over her pleasure spot and felt her release loom in the distance.

Xander's hand wrapped around his cock, and he began to gently pull at it. For several minutes they remained in silence, content to do nothing but watch one another pleasure themselves.

The reverie was broken was his deep voice commanded, "Come for me." Connie's mouth opened in a noiseless scream as her pleasure exploded, proving to her husband that she would indeed do whatever he asked of her.

Connie lay back on the stool trying to recover her breath when she felt his hands on her legs. Looking up, she saw that her husband had straddled the stool and she knew from the dark look in his eyes that she was about to be ravaged.

Reaching under her backside, Xander kneaded her buttocks for a moment before lifting them so that Connie sat astride him.

Wasting no time, he impaled her and began to rigorously thrust up into her. Having barely recovered from her first wave of pleasure, Connie sought to stall the second by lifting her hands to his face and kissing him.

Xander caught her hands in his and pulled them behind her back, holding them both in one of his large hands and causing her to arch her back. Connie looked down to see that her breasts bounced in time to each of his hard thrusts.

She began to roll her hips in time with his, but he held her still, demanding all the power as her hammered into her.

"I get bored by society affairs, Constance."

Connie barely comprehended his words as the sensations of his thrusts caused her pleasure to rise even higher.

"When I get inevitably bored, you're going to entertain me. Do you know what that means, flower?"

Oh god, yes!

"That first night was just a hint. You are going to get it harder and faster, Connie. I'm going to make you scream so loud."

Connie screamed in response, his words and actions combined sent her over the edge. She collapsed against him as his thrusts sped faster than she thought possible, and he spilled his seed inside her.

His torso held them both up as they fought to regain their breath. They gave one another sporadic kisses, pushing their lips against whatever skin they could reach.

With a groan, Xander released her hands so that he could grab her thighs and stand. She frantically wrapped her hands around his neck for balance as she felt him slip out of her.

After being gently laid on the bed, Connie's eyes fluttered shut as she stretched and sighed contentedly. She felt the bed dip beside her and a moment later felt his arms wrap around her as she was pulled against him.

"Have I mentioned that I love you?" Connie softly smiled at his words.

"Not in the last ten minutes." Murmurs of laughs spread from their lips.

Her eyelids drifted open to look up at him. He was smiling contentedly, if she did not know better, she would have said he was asleep. Resting her head on his bicep, she was happy to just lie in silence, looking at him.

"What are you thinking, petal?" His low voice permeated the air.

"Did you mean what you said just then?"

He opened his eyes to show a wicked glint in them. "I am afraid you will find yourself pulled behind many statues, curtains and hedges during our marriage."

"Well," Connie responded, "I imagine we shall be having rather a lot of fun then."

Epilogue

January 26th, 1810

"Would you please compose a letter to Harry, my love?" Looking down at the little bundle in her arms, Connie felt as though her heart was in a permanent state of melting.

The pair were currently in the bedroom of Xander's chambers in their country house. Connie was lying in the bed with Xander sat by her side. They had left her parents home for Bedfordshire in the early months of Autumn, deciding to return to his ancestral home before the journey would become too arduous for Connie.

They were pleased to discover on their return that the Dowager Countess had departed to continue her tradition of spending the off-season amongst her friends. She left behind a scathing note which did not have its intended effect as the pair could not help but laugh at the tedious insults thrown at them.

The following months were spent in peaceful bliss. Each day was dedicated to managing the estate and preparing for the arrival of their child whilst the nights were filled with passionate lovemaking.

"Harry? Not one hour old and you want me to leave the both of you to go write a letter." Xander laughed in response.

"'Tis only fair." Connie pleaded. "It may be years before he gets to meet his niece. Would it not be a small comfort for him to know that he is the first person we told?"

"And yet he will still be the last one to find out. Or will we wait to tell everyone else for several weeks until we hear back from him."

Taking her eyes off her daughter, Connie looked up at her husband, giggling. "Perhaps not my family but I would not be unhappy to delay in telling your mother."

Xander placed his hand over his heart in mock horror before reaching down to softly stroke his daughters head full of black hair. Connie sighed in joy at the sight.

"What do you think, little Una?" Xander tenderly asked the sleeping infant. "Should we hide you away for a while? Keep you all to ourselves?"

They could manage it, Connie thought, their families were miles away and unlikely to travel in the winter weather.

"Mama's last letter said they would be arriving in London next month. Can you imagine the surprise on their faces if we visited with this one in our arms?"

"Would that be the same mama who has birthed four children, petal?" Xander sweetly brushed a kiss against her brow. "I think she may have her suspicions by that point."

"It would be nice, though. To have our own little secret, if just for a short while."

Her husband leaned his head back in contemplation before answering. "Far be it for me to disobey the wishes of a new mother. I suppose if we did announce it right away, we would soon find our doors being beaten down."

"And a Wexford-Ainsworth duel would inevitably break out in the entrance hall." Connie tittered in response.

Resting her head upon her husband's shoulder, the pair sat in silence, content to simply look down at their little one and memorise and marvel at all her features.

Thinking back a year ago, Connie wondered at how her first season had exceeded all expectations. She had supposed that she would end up in a successful match, married off to a wealthy young man with a title. Yes, she had wed a wealthy young man with a title, but she was also blessed to marry a man who would manage to make her fall more in love with him with each passing day.

Gazing up at the man in question, Connie beamed at the look of utter astonishment on her husband's face.

"You know what this means, of course."

"Hmmm?" he sounded, not totally being brought out of his musings.

"As blessed as we are to have this beautiful creature, I shan't be happy until I provide you with an heir." His attention now completely focused on his wife as lust crossed his features. "As soon as I am able, we must put all our efforts into the task."

We dipped his head to nip at her ear before murmuring "Better to be safe, I shall settle for nothing less than an heir and a spare."

Connie shivered at his words and was astonished at how she could desire her husband so quickly after birth.

"But we have to wait." He moved away from her with a groan, standing and going to sit at the table beside the window.

"What are you doing?" Connie asked.

"What you told me to do!" Xander smirked. "Composing a letter to your warmongering brother."

Resting back against the pillows, Connie was comfortable to sit staring down at her daughter, the only sounds being the light scratch of the pen against paper as she wordlessly counted all her blessings and imagined the surprise on her brother's face when he learned of his niece's arrival.

What Connie did not know, however, was that the Wexford currently in her thoughts was preparing to write his own letter.

Sat in a cold officer's tent in the Spanish countryside, bundled up to protect himself from the chill, he reached for his pen, dipped it in the small pot of ink he had obtained that morning and began to write.

Dear Lady Eliza

COMING SOON

His Lordship's Star-Crossed Lady

Lady Eliza Ainsworth had always enjoyed thwarting expectations of her by constantly pushing the limits of what her parents could tolerate. It was therefore only natural that an invitation to dance by a scion of a rival family would be met with enthusiasm. What Eliza did not expect, however, was that the handsome young man would end up fuelling a desire she did not know she was capable of. When he left for war, she aimed to throw herself into the marriage mart, but would forgetting him be so easy?

Lord Harry Wexford thought that dancing with an Ainsworth would be a great way to irritate his brother, but the more he saw the woman, the more she invaded his thoughts and desires. Time and distance could not dampen the all-consuming need for her. Harry had to have her! The question was: Was she willing to risk losing her entire family to be with him?

ABOUT THE AUTHOR

Laura Osborne is excited to debut her first ever novel! After several years of enjoying reading romance novels, she decided to throw herself into the ring and with a degree in history, historical romance was the only way to go. She currently lives in South Wales where she is preparing to welcome her own little fur baby.

Printed in Great Britain
by Amazon

27689758R00185